LONGMAN CRITICAL ESSAYS

HAMLET

William Shakespeare

NORTH TYNESIDE COLLEGE
ENGLISH/COMMUNICATIONS
WORKSHOP

Editors:
Linda Cookson
Bryan Loughrey

Editors: Linda Cookson and Bryan Loughrey

Titles in the series:

CONTENTS

Like all professional groups, literary critics have developed their own specialised language. This is not necessarily a bad thing. Sometimes complex concepts can only be described in a terminology far removed from everyday speech. Academic jargon, however, creates an unnecessary barrier between the critic and the intelligent but less practised reader.

This danger is particularly acute where scholarly books and articles are re-packaged for a student audience. Critical anthologies, for example, often contain extracts from longer studies originally written for specialists. Deprived of their original context, these passages can puzzle and at times mislead. The essays in this volume, however, are all specially commissioned, self-contained works, written with the needs of students firmly in mind.

This is not to say that the contributors — all experienced critics and teachers — have in any way attempted to simplify the complexity of the issues with which they deal. On the contrary, they explore the central problems of the text from a variety of critical perspectives, reaching conclusions which are challenging and at times mutually contradictory.

They try, however, to present their arguments in a direct, accessible language and to work within the limitations of scope and length which students inevitably face. For this reason, essays are generally rather briefer than is the practice; they address quite specific topics; and, in line with examination requirements, they incorporate precise textual detail into the body of the discussion.

They offer, therefore, working examples of the kind of essay-writing skills which students themselves are expected to develop. Their diversity, however, should act as a reminder that in the field of literary studies there is no such thing as a 'model' answer. Good essays are the outcome of a creative engagement with literature, of sensitive, attentive reading and careful thought. We hope that those contained in this volume will encourage students to return to the most important starting point of all, the text itself, with renewed excitement and the determination to explore more fully their own critical responses.

How to use this volume

Obviously enough, you should start by reading the text in question. The one assumption that all the contributors make is that you are already familiar with this. It would be helpful, of course, to have read further — perhaps other works by the same author or by influential contemporaries. But we don't assume that you have yet had the opportunity to do this and any references to historical background or to other works of literature are explained.

You should, perhaps, have a few things to hand. It is always a good idea to keep a copy of the text nearby when reading critical studies. You will almost certainly want to consult it when checking the context of quotations or pausing to consider the validity of the critic's interpretation. You should also try to have access to a good dictionary, and ideally a copy of a dictionary of literary terms as well. The contributors have tried to avoid jargon and to express themselves clearly and directly. But inevitably there will be occasional words or phrases with which you are unfamiliar. Finally, we would encourage you to make notes, summarising not just the argument of each essay but also your own responses to what you have read. So keep a pencil and notebook at the ready.

Suitably equipped, the best thing to do is simply begin with whichever topic most interests you. We have deliberately organised each volume so that the essays may be read in any order. One consequence of this is that, for the sake of clarity and self-containment, there is occasionally a degree of overlap between essays. But at least you are not forced to follow one — fairly arbitrary — reading sequence.

Each essay is followed by brief 'Afterthoughts', designed to highlight points of critical interest. But remember, these are only there to remind you that it is *your* responsibility to question what you read. The essays printed here are not a series of 'model' answers to be slavishly imitated and in no way should they be regarded as anything other than a guide or stimulus for your own thinking. We hope for a critically involved response: 'That was interesting. But if *I* were tackling the topic . . .!'

Read the essays in this spirit and you'll pick up many of the skills of critical composition in the process. We have, however, tried to provide more explicit advice in 'A practical guide to essay writing'. You may find this helpful, but do not imagine it offers any magic formulas. The quality of your essays ultimately depends on the quality of your engagement with literary texts. We hope this volume spurs you on to read these with greater understanding and to explore your responses in greater depth.

A note on the text

All references are to the New Penguin Shakespeare edition of *Hamlet*, ed. T J B Spencer.

Peter Reynolds

Peter Reynolds is Lecturer in Drama at the Roehampton Institute of Higher Education, and author of Text into Performance *(Penguin, 1985).*

ESSAY

Hamlet Act I, scene 1 — the art of dramatic exposition

Let us remind ourselves of the obvious: we are not studying a novel or a poem but a play. The printed text in front of us is therefore incomplete and much work remains for the reader to do; for, unlike a novel or a poem, a play is unfinished even when it appears in a bookshop in glossy covers set in impressive-looking typeface. Shakespeare may have completed his *Hamlet* around 1603, or rather he may have completed writing the words he hoped would be spoken by the actors in the Lord Chamberlain's Men. But once that task was completed, what then existed in manuscript (and later in print) was not *the* play, but a series of complex instructions as to how a play might eventually be made. This condition is not unique to the work of Shakespeare: the text of any dramatist is incomplete and partial without the added dimension of performance. To add to that dimension is the task of 'active' readers. They must create a performance text in the theatre of the mind's eye in order to complete for themselves what the playwright begins. To do this requires an alliance of the intellect and the informed imagination, and the willingness of the reader to be prepared to emulate the performer.

Although dramatists can control what they commit to paper, they cannot control the process in the theatre whereby what is written is translated by others into what is performed. There are things which cannot be written down and spoken by actors, but which can be *shown* in performance to an audience. What is said by actors, those words a dramatist has written for them to say, does not exist in a vacuum, but in a given performance context. The active reader must attempt to *contextualise* the dramatist's written text in imaginary or recalled performance. The context of that performance will generate its own text which acts and reacts upon what was originally written by Shakespeare. The resulting performance text will take into account such factors as the physical location of actors and the groupings they contrive to make; their costumes and gestural language; the colours used in a designer's setting; and the objects or props employed as expressions of the personalities being enacted or as tools in the furtherance of the action. Performance context is also manufactured by those whose task it is literally to translate dramatic literature into theatrical event: by actors, directors, designers and, not least, by audiences. Active readers must recall, in reading what is printed to be spoken, that words themselves are *not* sovereign in the context of performance. They are part of a larger discourse.

One of the most difficult things for any writer to do well is the opening paragraphs of a new work. If the reader is put off at the outset, it is unlikely that what follows will receive much attention. This is even more true in the theatre. There, when the lights in the auditorium dim, the audience's intense focus on the stage can soon be dissipated and lost if the clues on the printed page have not been effectively deciphered and translated by the performers into theatre-language.

How, then, does Shakespeare choose to organise his opening material?

Part of Shakespeare's continuing success as a dramatic writer seems to me to lie in his recognition that audiences like variety. His plays never seem static, but have a fluid quality which constantly changes the nature of the appeal to the eye and the ear. The truth of this statement is clearly apparent when the structure of the opening scene is examined. It divides readily into three parts. The opening section begins at the moment when the audience are made collectively to focus on the guard Francisco, and lasts until the Ghost has made his first exit. What distinguishes this series of actions from subsequent ones is that the pace, once the spoken text comes into play, is uniformly brisk. The short staccato sentences of Barnardo and Francisco mark a sense of urgency in their exchange. Likewise the pace of the language is reinforced by the rapid movements off and on to the stage (Barnardo enters, followed by Horatio and Marcellus, whilst Francisco exits), and the entry of the fifth actor, the Ghost, signals a new urgency as the other characters onstage and the audience struggle to discover what it is and what it wants.

The second section of the scene begins after the Ghost exits for the first time and continues until it is seen for the second time, around line 125. This mid-section of the scene is longer than the other two. It is also, if you look at it carefully, much calmer in atmosphere and more deliberate than the first.

The passage contains less physical action (no one enters or leaves the stage), but there is more talk and more listening. The language itself is different from section one. The initial abrupt sentences are now replaced by much longer phrases, and actors speak without interruption for several minutes at a time instead of for a matter of seconds. Again, there are clues in the words themselves to the enactment of the performance. Shakespeare provides linguistic signals which establish the mood and simultaneously help to make the transition between sections. Thus the key words of the opening section seem to me to be, 'cold', 'silent', and 'sick'. But in section two the language is more cool and reflective. It is legalistic, full of references to 'sealed compact[s]', 'inheritance', things 'well ratified by law and heraldry'. Most of the time, the actors reinforce the almost-reflective mood and slower pace by themselves being still, sitting and listening to what is being said.

The third and final section of the scene begins when the second entry of the Ghost shatters the relative calm of the middle section and scatters the seated actors across the stage. Although the entrance is a shock for the audience, the foundations for it have already been laid. Firstly, there is the use by

Shakespeare of a particular *grouping* of the actors. Just before the Ghost's first entrance, Barnardo asks the others to sit. It is whilst they are thus literally off-guard that the Ghost makes his entrance. Now, following their unsuccessful challenge to old Hamlet, the group of Barnardo, Marcellus and Horatio is left alone again, and this time it is Marcellus who asks them to sit. Quite simply, what this is designed to achieve is the triggering of the audience's visual memory: the last time the Ghost had appeared followed an identical movement. When it is repeated, they anticipate a similar immediate response. The gesture of sitting quickens anticipation. This is built upon by the change in language that gradually occurs in Horatio's spoken text: between lines 112 and 125 he moves from contemplation of the dry facts of his world's current political realities to a thrilling story of the historical and mythical past. Here the key words are 'blood', 'disasters' and 'doomsday'. Incidentally, the fact that Horatio uses such 'theatrical' language to describe the events surrounding the assassination of Julius Caesar suggests that Shakespeare may have intended his first audiences to recall their own theatrical memory of those events presented on the stage of the Globe some two years previously.

Once the Ghost manifests itself for the second time, the pace of the action immediately quickens. Horatio desperately, and with increasing frustration, repeats his demand, 'Speak to me'; while attempts by the other players to strike at the apparition with their weapons indicate a fast and flowing movement around the stage. The characters are, paradoxically, in some way enlivened by this creature from the dead; each abandons a sedentary position to assume an active role. The entrance releases a tremendous amount of energy — energy which, despite a slight lessening of the subsequent pace, sets up a momentum which will carry the action on to the end of the scene. Marcellus, Barnardo, Horatio (*and* the audience) may initially have been frustrated in their desire to find out the significance of the Ghost's appearance, but they have lost none of their desire to know what it is. What is more, Horatio now offers a key which seems to have the power to unlock some of the secrets posed by the action of the first scene: now, and only now, at the end of this extraordinary series of events, is the name 'Hamlet' brought to the ears of eager listeners. The group assembled on stage are told, and thus the audience learns, that 'This spirit, dumb to us, will speak to him'.

Further clues to the shape and pace of the scene can be found in references to the passing of time. If you look carefully at each section you will see that stage-time is compressed in section one, elongated in section two, and compressed again in the last section. These changes are very necessary dramatically. An audience cannot remain indefinitely in a heightened state of excitement and expectation, and certainly not for the three hours and more of playing-time taken up by most productions of *Hamlet*. Therefore, in this first scene, and throughout the play, moments of high tension are inevitably followed by periods of relative calm. There are times when the audience needs to be involved in the action, and times when it needs to be able to reflect on the *significance* of that action. This kind of ebb and flow of the dramatic text is reflected in changes in stage-time. Scene one manipulates time and relies on different chronological schemes for much of its power and ability to indicate significance. The scene itself takes twenty minutes to enact, but those twenty minutes encompass a shift in stage-time from before midnight to dawn. As you will recall, the action of the first section is brisk. In keeping with this there needs to be only enough actual compression of stage-time to move a little over one hour: from before midnight, to midnight itself ('tis now struck twelve'), through to one o'clock (the Ghost, we learn, last appeared when the bell struck one, and presumably does so again). The second and slower-paced section covers, appropriately enough, a much longer period of stage-time. It moves from shortly after one o'clock in the morning, to just before the break of dawn, probably nearly four hours in perhaps ten or twelve minutes of playing time. The final section takes us from that time just before dawn, signalled by the crowing cock ('the trumpet to the morn' is, like the bell, an interesting and effective use of a sound effect), to Horatio's sighting of dawn itself ('But look, the morn in russet mantle clad/ Walks o'er the dew of yon high eastward hill' — lines 167–168), and finally on to the very last line of the last section, where Marcellus establishes that it is now morning. At the end of the scene, the language becomes more poetic, and there is a sense of optimism and purpose that goes hand-in-hand with the light of day.

References to night and day are not without significance in this opening scene. You might ask yourself why the first piece of spoken text in *Hamlet* is a question. Why does Barnardo need to ask, 'Who's there?' Does he not recognise Francisco? In fact, each character appears to need time to identify the other. This may indicate that in the original performances both actors wore costumes including a helmet with a visor which, when down, covered the face. Such costuming would suggest that this guard is one in which it is necessary to be armed to the teeth. But the question also says something about the time. Shakespeare is signalling to the audience that the scene is taking place at night, and the actors take time to see one another because they need to *demonstrate* to their audience, who during the Jacobean period would be watching in broad daylight, that on the stage, it is dark. The conversation is strengthened and confirmed aurally when Barnardo actually announces the time of day. To make it quite clear, he says not only that it has 'now struck twelve', but that it is also time for Franscisco to go to bed.

Other questions you should perhaps ask yourself concern the Ghost. What should it look like? How should it be represented? This 'character' poses problems almost as difficult as those surrounding the presentation of the Witches in *Macbeth*. There is of course a danger that contemporary audiences (and readers) will not take the appearance of such paranormal phenomena as 'real', but simply see them as a rather hackneyed use of a familiar Elizabethan stage convention. It is important that we remember that, to the Elizabethans, ghosts were not part of a distant and faintly amusing folklore, but accepted as real presences in the real world. This point is amply illustrated by the reaction which greeted a near-contemporary performance of Christopher Marlowe's *Doctor Faustus* in Exeter. A riot almost ensued because of the appearance onstage of one too many 'devils'. However familiar the Elizabethans may have been with the appearance of ghosts on their stages, they were never completely sanguine or blasé about them. In recent times, when the actor Jonathan Pryce played Hamlet in a production by Richard Eyre at London's Royal Court Theatre, the Ghost was never actually seen onstage at all (the opening scene I have been analysing was cut entirely), but was represented simply and effectively as a disembodied voice which seemed to come from within the body of Hamlet himself. It was as if the Prince were possessed. It is interesting to note that Hamlet himself, in what he says, never questions the *existence* of the Ghost, although he does reflect on the nature of 'this thing' (The spirit that I have seen/ May be a devil, and the devil hath power/ T'assume a pleasing shape' — II.2.596–598). Whatever *you* decide, you should not avoid the problems of representing the supernatural. The printed text does provide a clue as to how Shakespeare himself wanted the Ghost to be seen: Horatio indicates that the Ghost is wearing armour. Whether or not you decide to see in your mind's eye an actor wearing actual armour, you must, I think, show a man in military uniform. This ghost is that of a king ready for war, and not one clad in ceremonial robes of state. The printed text also offers a clue to reinforce the visual impression: the actor playing the role should adopt, as Marcellus points out, a 'martial stalk'.

The whole opening of this scene operates as one over-whelming question. Something, we are forced to accept, is indeed wrong in this state of Denmark, but *what*? The real stagecraft lies in not merely making the audience aware in their conscious minds that all is not well, but in making them *feel* and *experience* the unease that so completely engulfs the characters, and foregrounds Hamlet standing ready to resolve the mystery. What a wonderful preparation for the entrance of an actor this scene is: no wonder to act the role is the dream and ambition of most young actors.

So much is achieved in the beginning of this play which makes the actor's part possible. Mood, atmosphere, tension, time, place, anticipation are generated by a *combination* of signals, only some of which exist in the printed text. The rest must be determined by the imagination and judgement of you, the active reader.

AFTERTHOUGHTS

1

What does Reynolds mean by 'active' readers (pages 9–10)?

2

Reynolds states that there are 'things which cannot be written down and spoken by actors, but which can be *shown* in performance to an audience' (page 10). What do you imagine he has in mind here?

3

Are there any advantages to reading a play rather than seeing it?

4

Reynolds comments (page 13) that 'There are times when the audience needs to be involved in the action, and times when it needs to be able to reflect on the *significance* of that action'. At what points in this scene do you feel that an audience should 'reflect'?

John Cunningham

John Cunningham divides his time between travel and writing. He is the author of numerous critical studies.

ESSAY

Is *Hamlet* a problem play?

Hamlet presents problems to us all: to the editor, the producer and the actor — and their problems are all of importance to the student or the critic, who must try to arrive at a justifiable view of the central character and of the nature and themes of the play.

The editor is faced with a choice of three texts. The 'bad Quarto' piratically published in 1603, which may represent an early version of the finished work, was followed in 1604 by the 'good Quarto', whose text is the usual basis of modern editions; but the First Folio of 1623, brought out after Shakespeare's death by two of his friends, is some two hundred lines shorter than the Second Quarto. As we shall see, the problems created by the existence of the rival texts are not merely for scholars, but have relevance to anyone trying to understand the play.

The length of the 'accepted' text may well be the producer's first difficulty. *Hamlet* is a long play compared with many of its author's other works, and contains a number of characters whose parts are very small. Producers might well ask themselves if they could cut out the single appearance of Reynaldo — but this would obscure a very unpleasant aspect of Polonius, who is seen to spy on his own son; they may remove both Voltimand and Cornelius — thus reducing the importance of the political background to the story, the diplomatic skill shown by Claudius in diverting attention to his strong foreign policy; perhaps this might lead the way to the removal altogether of Fortinbras, who appears once with his army without speaking and then pops up at the very end to take over the troubled kingdom and speak Hamlet's epitaph. But that epitaph is as important as it may be unexpected — he says Hamlet deserves a soldier's funeral, and it is a soldier who is speaking — and Fortinbras is necessary to make up the complement of four men each of whom represents one of the 'humours' which were the way in which character was then interpreted. Hamlet is melancholy, Horatio is phlegmatic, Laertes is choleric and Fortinbras, from all we hear of him, is sanguine, the outgoing man of action in direct contrast to the leading role.

The producer must decide on a number of other practical issues. Does Hamlet know he is overheard in the 'get thee to a nunnery' passage (III.1.89–150)? If so, is the cue 'Where's your father?' or the question (highly insulting to a girl) 'Are you honest?' Is his madness to be taken as an assumed 'antic disposition', as he describes it, or is it to be presented as in part a reflection of his own instability — he behaves quite wildly not only after seeing the Ghost, but also after the success of his plot with the play. Is Polonius to be played for laughs, or are we to see the more sinister person over whose body his killer can casually say 'Thou findest to be too busy is some danger' (III.4.34)? Are Rosencrantz and Guildenstern harmless stooges, or more sinister agents of whom Hamlet can truly say 'they did make love to this employment' after he has arranged their death? These are a few of the questions which have to be settled in directing the actors.

The person who acts the hero obviously has the greatest problems. He must decide such elementary things as whether Hamlet is thin and bookish in appearance, or fat, as he is called in the duel scene — though he is sweating at the time, and the word may mean no more. Crucially, he must decide how old he is. He is always called 'young Hamlet' but this is either by older people or by friends who are distinguishing between him and his father, whose name was the same. Yet in the graveyard scene Shakespeare seems to go out of his way to insist that he is about thirty — the gravedigger began work the day Hamlet was born, and has been digging for thirty years; and Hamlet can well remember Yorick, who has lain in the earth, we are told, 'three-and-twenty years'. And if Hamlet is thirty, what does that *mean*? Thirty in the year 1600 was not the same as thirty today. If his mother married and bore him at the minimum age, she must be in her mid-forties: it is tempting to put a modern gloss on her and see her, in her rash love-affair, as a menopausal woman clutching at a last chance of passion, but in Shakespeare's day she would have been old. Hamlet's age, then, will affect more than one actor. So too will his attitude to women in general, about which we shall have more to say later; but he certainly behaves oddly both to his mother and to Ophelia, and the actor in the end must decide whether he really loves (more than 'forty thousand brothers', as he tells Laertes) the girl whom he treats so cruelly with his bawdy jests in public during the performance of the play at court, and whom he distresses so much with his assumed madness. Above all, Hamlet must try to answer what many people regard as the central question of the play: the actor must ask himself 'Why do I delay? I am told in Act I my whole duty is to carry out due vengeance for my father, and I finally do so — after reproving myself many times for my failure — in the closing moments of the play, when I am near to death myself. Why so long?' This affects the whole performance of the part, and nowhere is it more difficult in practice than in the 'prayer' scene, when he has the opportunity to kill the King unguarded, and does not do so.

This problem — Hamlet's refusal to take action — is by many critics regarded as the central one; but the student of the play must bear in mind all the other questions which have been raised, before he can hope to arrive at his own explanation.

What choice, then, have we in trying to answer the supposed 'central' question, and so coming to an acceptable interpretation of the whole play?

We may begin by considering the simplest and oldest. When the author was a young man, there was a revival of interest in the plays of Seneca, a Roman author of dramas apparently meant to be read rather than acted, full of bloody action, supernatural elements and commonly turning on the theme of revenge. Stripped to its elements — and this is where that notorious 'bad Quarto' is of interest — *Hamlet* may be seen as following this pattern. The long-runner of the Elizabethan stage (today's longest run, interestingly enough, takes its title from Hamlet, who calls his own production *The Mousetrap*) was Kyd's *The Spanish Tragedy*, and that is a gory story of revenge — in fact, it is *Hamlet* turned inside out, a father being charged to avenge his son. Perhaps we have here no more than a type of play the audience knew as well as we know a Western or an International Spy film plot: it is simply a matter of how much trouble the dramatist put into the writing. However, if we compare this play with Shakespeare's most clearly 'Senecan' effort — *Titus Andronicus* — we are likely to feel that the genre was altogether too crude to convey the sort of intellectual subtlety that we find in *Hamlet*.

Young students, in particular, may find the 'romantic' Hamlet more acceptable. Early in the nineteenth century, many romantic writers saw in this play a reflection of what they believed themselves to be: young, eager and earnest, but coming into conflict with the corrupt world of the older generation, suffering deep disillusionment and almost seeking death, as Keats said he did and Shelley did in fact. Hamlet can indeed be played as an adolescent, quite successfully: his rage against the political world which has cheated him of his right, his obsession with his mother's sexuality, his failure to achieve a real relationship with Ophelia — and, of course, the many references to his youth which we have already noted — all contribute to a convincing presentation. And as we are told repeatedly that he is a 'student' we can make him an undergraduate.

But clearly he was not — graduation would be of no significance to a royal prince — and we may assume that he was simply an intellectual man who liked intellectual company, a good library and so on, all of which were to be found in university towns. But this brings us to a third, carefully argued and still highly popular interpretation, first put forward in 1904 by A C Bradley. The basis of this idea is to assume what has been implied in the opening of this paragraph: that the character may be thought of as an actual person, living a real life, not merely existing on the stage. Bradley developed, with great eloquence, an idea as old as Aristotle, who said that the hero of a tragedy must not be perfect because we could not feel for him if he were — he must have a 'human' weakness, or we cannot in any way identify with him and feel for his suffering. Bradley extends this notion of what is often called the 'tragic flaw' to all of Shake-speare's major tragic heroes: thus Othello's flaw is jealousy, Macbeth's is ambition and Hamlet's, of course, is indecision. There are two objections to this concept. Aristotle held that the 'flaw' in all heroes, indeed in all men, is the same: it is the special kind of pride which the Greeks called *hubris*, which means that pride which persuades men that they are really in control of the world; in short that they are God. Hamlet, seen in this light, is guilty of questioning the workings of fate, of doubting the validity of the Ghost, of setting himself up as the interpreter of destiny. The other objection is that the characters in a play, however well drawn, do not in fact exist outside the scenes in which they appear. Pushed to its logical limits, this view means that we start asking ourselves what Hamlet studied at Wittenberg, and considering what a post-mortem on Ophelia might show that she had had for her breakfast on the morning of her death. Yet this concept of character is still very widely held, and much critical writing on *Hamlet* is based firmly upon it: so it is urged that Hamlet delays in killing the King simply because he is never physically able to do so, except in the 'prayer' scene. This is to talk about him as though he had a physical existence. If his creator had wanted him to have other opportunities, he would quite simply have written them in.

The ultimate — and famous — extension of this view is that propounded by a psychoanalyst, the distinguished biographer of Freud, Dr Ernest Jones, who wrote an influential account of Hamlet as though he existed so truly that he could be subjected to analysis. He said that Hamlet was a case-book example of the Oedipus complex, that form of arrested sexual development in men in which they fail to transfer their first attachment, to their mothers, to other women. Sufferers tend to remain in a state of adolescence, and often fail to come to terms with the 'real' world, whatever that might be. There is quite a lot of evidence for this view in the play — Dr Jones was no mean scholar. Hamlet does indeed have a most equivocal relationship with Ophelia, to whom he promises '*almost* all the holy vows of heaven' (I.3.14 — author's italics) — that is, he cannot bring himself to commit himself fully — and whom he later treats with revulsion in the 'get thee to a nunnery' scene; he also seems obsessed with his mother's sexual behaviour, to which he refers in very specific detail in his great scene in her private room, even urging her not to have intercourse with her husband and advising her how to curb her desire to do so; and it is typical of this psychological state that the son should resent to an extreme the presence of another man in his mother's life, as is here the case.

When Olivier made his popular film of the play in 1948, it was this interpretation that he presented. Preceding the action by saying that it was about a man 'who could not make up his mind', he went on to emphasise any line which might support the Oedipus explanation, helped not a little by the fact that the actress playing his mother was, in reality, younger than he! The most important aspect of this performance for our purposes is that it worked very well — it was consistent within its own limits, and an effective interpretation.

A final choice is offered to all of us who seek to unravel this play. An American critic, E E Stoll, partly in reaction to the conventional 'character-analysis' school of thought, proposed that we are entirely wrong in studying the play at all, which was thought of, by its author, simply as an afternoon's perform-ance. The crowd in the playhouse would not be studying the quirks of character that are found by the student, would not notice the 'inconsistencies' in Hamlet's behaviour which we have laboured long to resolve, would not ask why he delayed: if he had not delayed, but 'swept to his revenge', there would be either no play or a mere one-acter, and an Elizabethan audi-ence wanted much more. This is an extreme view, but it is worth thinking about seriously. After all, some of the other views we have been looking at are rather far out — Hamlet as Eternal Youth, for example; and no doubt there is a Marxist *Hamlet*, since there is certainly a strong case for thinking of the play as about power or politics.

Is Hamlet, then, young or middle-aged? Is he irresolute, or ruthless, postponing his revenge only until he is certain of its validity and sure that he will damn his victim to hell, not catch him at his prayers? Is he, as Fortinbras and Ophelia both tell us, a man of soldierly qualities, or a broody, withdrawn de-pressive; is he obsessed by sexual jealousy or disgusted by the world's corruption, as his fastidious nature appears to be disgusted by drunkenness? Is he Revenge incarnate or a complex, academic 'perpetual student'? Is he 'passion's slave'? Is he no more than a character in a play, a rehash of an old melodrama, who acts as he does because the needs of the theatre so dictate?

Perhaps the answer lies in the last question. *Hamlet* is a play. It is one of those rare stories which every age interprets anew. It has been acted in many different ways, and all of them seem to work. What we are dealing with is not so much a problem as a mystery — how could a hard-working and hard-headed dramatist take a rubbishy old yarn and make out of it a work which assumes new life for each generation that comes to it?

AFTERTHOUGHTS

1

How important is it to know Hamlet's age?

2

What are the problems of thinking of Hamlet as a real person? Are there any advantages to this approach?

3

Cunningham comments that there is 'a strong case for thinking of the play as about power or politics' (page 22). What case could you make to support this claim?

4

This essay looks at the word 'problem' in its general sense. What relevance might the specialist term 'Problem Play' have to *Hamlet*, however?

Alan Gardiner

Alan Gardiner has been a GCE examiner for several years and is a Lecturer in English Language and Literature at Redbridge Technical College. He is the author of several critical studies.

ESSAY

The state of Denmark

The world of *Hamlet* is a remarkably enclosed one. From the opening scene, which introduces us to a society heavily fortified against attack from without, to the close of the play the action remains concentrated at Elsinore. The frequent references to other places — to Paris, Wittenberg, Norway, Poland and England — merely underline the play's restricted use of location. Characters do leave Denmark but we see nothing of them until they return. Correspondingly, characters from the world outside Denmark only enter the play when the action brings them to Elsinore: the Players have travelled from another city and probably from another country, and Fortinbras's appearance is delayed until his expedition against the Poles takes him through Danish territory. The society depicted in the play is oppressively narrow and claustrophobic; for the audience as well as for Hamlet, Denmark is indeed something of a prison.

The first scene also suggests that this society is a deeply disturbed one. Even before the silent movement of the Ghost across the stage 'harrows' Horatio 'with fear and wonder' there is a feeling of uneasiness and apprehension in the tense, nervous exchanges between the guards; the unsettled atmosphere is such that Francisco feels 'sick at heart'. Horatio believes the coming of the Ghost 'bodes some strange eruption to our state' and Marcellus's account of the country's urgent preparations for war increases the sense of a troubled kingdom. Another important function of this scene is to suggest the nature of the old order which existed in Denmark when Hamlet's father was alive, an order which has been superseded by a very different set of values now that Claudius is on the throne. 'Valiant Hamlet' emerges as a man of honour who settled disputes such as that with Fortinbras (the elder) of Norway by personal combat. The appearance of the King's Ghost, 'majestical' and of 'fair and warlike form', similarly suggests a heroic figure.

In contrast to the cold, menacing darkness of the play's opening, the scene which follows presents the light, warmth and formal splendour of Claudius's court. However, although at this stage we know nothing of the murder he has committed to win the throne, Claudius's very first speech hints at the corruption beneath his dignified exterior. The elaborate phrasing of the opening sixteen lines betrays a desire to gloss over the unseemliness of his marriage to his brother's sister — a marriage which has not only been entered into with unbecoming haste but which would also, in Shakespeare's time, have been regarded as incestuous:

> Therefore our sometime sister, now our Queen,
> Th'imperial jointress to this warlike state,
> Have we, as 'twere with a defeated joy,
> With an auspicious, and a dropping eye,
> With mirth in funeral, and with dirge in marriage,
> In equal scale weighing delight and dole,
> Taken to wife.

(I.2.8–14)

The revelation that Claudius is a usurper and guilty of fratricide confirms that he is the principal source of the rottenness which pervades Denmark. He is an efficient ruler (his competent handling of the threat from Fortinbras is an early illustration of this), but throughout the play his actions are governed by a ruthless self-interest; his conscience may trouble him, but guilt is not allowed to influence the execution of policy. His reaction to Hamlet's murder of Polonius is characteristic. His first thought is that the victim might have been himself ('It had been so with us, had we been there'), and he then acts swiftly to ensure the outrage does not weaken his position as king: his wish is that 'slander' should 'miss our name'. (IV.1). He is a skilful manipulator of others, persuading Rosencrantz and Guildenstern to betray their friendship with Hamlet and succeeding first in calming Laertes and then in inducing him to cooperate in the plot against Hamlet. This plot involves a cynical exploitation of Hamlet's open, trusting nature; Claudius knows he will not inspect the foils because he is 'Most generous, and free from all contriving' (IV.7.134).

Claudius's court is populated by figures who endorse his values, either by actively living their lives according to the same principles or by a passive acceptance of the status quo. The character most clearly at home in this society is Polonius. He has happily transferred his allegiance to the new regime and assures Claudius:

> I hold my duty as I hold my soul,
> Both to my God and to my gracious King.

(II.2.44–45)

In his words of advice to Laertes before the latter returns to France (I.3.58–80), he preaches a cynical doctrine of calculation ('Give thy thoughts to tongue,/ Nor any unproportioned thought his act'), wariness of others ('Give every man thine ear, but few thy voice') and self-interest. In the same scene he similarly warns Ophelia against the spontaneous expression of emotion, rebuking her for too 'free and bounteous' a response to Hamlet's overtures (I.3.93). He pours scorn on his daughter's faith in the honesty of Hamlet's declarations of love: 'Affection? Pooh! You speak like a green girl' (I.3.101). In Polonius's scheme of things a love relationship is much like a financial transaction, and should be conducted with a similar cold objectivity ('you have ta'en these tenders for true pay,/ Which are not sterling. Tender yourself more dearly .../ Set your entreatments at a higher rate' — I.3.106–107, 122). His distrust of others extends even to his own son, whom Reynaldo is sent to spy upon. Such deviousness is typical of Polonius, who employs similar methods on several other occasions in the play. He reads Ophelia's letters from Hamlet, reporting the contents to the King, and uses his daughter as bait so that he and Claudius can secretly observe Hamlet's manner towards her. It is his readiness to spy upon others that finally brings about his downfall. His reason for listening behind the arras when Hamlet meets Gertrude is characteristically distasteful:

> 'Tis meet that some more audience than a mother
> (Since nature makes them partial) should o'erhear
> The speech of vantage.

(III.3.31–33)

Polonius's son proves capable of still baser duplicity. That Laertes shares his father's cynicism is evident early in the play, when he too speaks dismissively of Hamlet's love for Ophelia, urging his sister to withhold her affection and trust: 'For Hamlet, and the trifling of his favour,/ Hold it a fashion . . ./ The perfume and suppliance of a minute . . ./ Be wary, then. Best safety lies in fear' (I.3.5–9, 43). When he returns from France and seeks immediate vengeance for his father's death he is clearly to be seen as a contrast to Hamlet, but he is equally clearly not presented as an example the audience would wish Hamlet to follow. Untroubled by moral scruples ('Conscience and grace to the profoundest pit!' — IV.5.134), he would be willing to murder Hamlet in church and compounds the treachery of Claudius's plot by proposing that he use a poisoned foil in the fencing match.

Like Laertes, Rosencrantz and Guildenstern become the willing instruments of a corrupt king, abandoning the principles of friendship in order to assist Claudius's manoeuvrings against Hamlet. Their fellow courtier Osric is a comic illustration of the kind of mindless servitude that enables Claudius to remain in power. The women in the play have a finer sensitivity than these characters but they too are pawns in the intrigues devised by Claudius and Polonius. Ophelia at first defends Hamlet when her father questions his sincerity, but she obeys when she is told to avoid further contact with him. She also gives up Hamlet's letters to her and allows Polonius and the King to listen in when she meets him — a meeting that has been deliberately set up by her father. Gertrude, because of her marriage to Claudius, is more actively corrupt, though this is offset by her genuine compassion for her son and by her acknowledgement of her own guilt when Hamlet confronts her with it. But she stands by as Claudius and Polonius plot and scheme and she raises no objection to Polonius hiding behind the arras when she speaks to

Hamlet in her room.

The Danish royal court, then, is full of characters who readily acquiesce in, if they do not actively promote, the corruption of their king. It is unsurprising that the Council's 'better wisdoms' have 'freely' supported Claudius's accession and incestuous marriage (I.2.14–16). Denmark emerges as a society in which spying, manipulation and deceit are norms of human behaviour — a place where 'one may smile, and smile, and be a villain' (I.5.108). The pleasures of the court are of an appropriately coarse and dissolute nature:

> This heavy-headed revel east and west
> Makes us traduced and taxed of other nations.
> They clepe us drunkards, and with swinish phrase
> Soil our addition.

> (I.4.17–20)

Hamlet here attributes drunkenness not just to Claudius's inner circle but to the Danish people as a whole, and elsewhere in the play there are further suggestions that the rottenness in Denmark extends beyond the court. The people are described as 'muddied,/ Thick and unwholesome in their thoughts and whispers' (IV.5.82–83). Hamlet comments on the fickleness evident in their transference of allegiance from his father to Claudius: those who used to make faces at Claudius now pay money for pictures of him (II.2.62–65). At other points in the play we are told that they support Hamlet (said to be 'loved of the distracted multitude' — IV.3.4) and then Laertes, who is accompanied by a 'rabble' of 'false Danish dogs' when he storms the court (IV.5.104, 112).

A profound sickness afflicts the whole society, and gives rise to the play's recurring imagery of foulness, rottenness and disease. Inevitably, these images are frequently centred upon Claudius: when he is attempting to pray he admits that his crime is 'rank' and 'smells to heaven' (III.3.6), and in the same scene Hamlet spares his life, with the comment, 'This physic but prolongs thy sickly days' (III.3.96). It is appropriate to the portrayal of a society riddled with deceit, and in which important elements of the nation's sickness (such as Claudius's murder of his brother) are hidden from general view, that the disease imagery should often suggest an infection attacking the body from within. In the closet scene, Hamlet urges his mother not to attribute his words to madness and so overlook her own sinful behaviour:

> It will but skin and film the ulcerous place,
> Whiles rank corruption, mining all within,
> Infects unseen.
>
> (III.4.148–150)

Young Fortinbras's dispute with Poland is compared by Hamlet to:

> ... th'imposthume of much wealth and peace,
> That inward breaks, and shows no cause without
> Why the man dies.
>
> (IV.4.27–29)

Such images can be linked with the play's repeated emphasis on the discrepancy between, again in Hamlet's words, what 'seems' and what 'is'. Polonius speaks of how with 'pious action we do sugar o'er/ The devil himself', and this prompts Claudius's aside:

> The harlot's cheek, beautied with plastering art,
> Is not more ugly to the thing that helps it
> Than is my deed to my most painted word.
>
> (III.1.51–53)

But in the course of the play the corruption of Denmark is progressively uncovered, a development that is anticipated at the close of the second scene:

> Foul deeds will rise,
> Though all the earth o'erwhelm them, to men's eyes.
>
> (I.2.257–258)

The widespread sickness of the society is one reason for the enthusiasm and affection with which Hamlet greets those characters who are newly arrived in Denmark and therefore likely to be untainted by its corruption. The Players receive such a welcome, as do Horatio (who has come from Wittenberg) and Rosencrantz and Guildenstern (who have been summoned by the King, possibly from Wittenberg also). Hamlet soon discovers that Rosencrantz and Guildenstern are in Elsinore to serve the

King's purposes, but Horatio is a friend who is worthy of his trust. For the audience also, Horatio's loyalty and honesty are a refreshing contrast to the prevalent duplicity, servility and self-interest. Unlike Hamlet, however, Horatio is never a threat to the established order of Denmark. Hamlet's observation that 'There are more things in heaven and earth, Horatio,/ Than are dreamt of in your philosophy' (I.5.166–167) suggests Horatio's limited perception; he lacks Hamlet's insight into the rottenness that surrounds them.

Hamlet's disgust at the nature of life in Elsinore is shared by no one but the audience. From the second scene, when his soliloquy uncovers the ugly reality beneath the pageantry and splendour of Claudius's court, Hamlet is our guide to the world of the play and Shakespeare offers ample evidence to support his view of it:

> . . . 'tis an unweeded garden
> That grows to seed. Things rank and gross in nature
> Possess it merely.

(I.2.135–137)

Moreover, the finer aspects of Hamlet's character highlight the human deficiencies of the rest of the court; he possesses the very qualities that Claudius and Polonius denigrate and reject — qualities such as openness, honesty and spontaneity. Hamlet is oppressed by an overwhelming despair and disgust but we see enough warmth, humour and generosity (in his exchanges with Horatio and the Players, for example) to convince us of his essential goodness. There is also Ophelia's description:

> O, what a noble mind is here o'erthrown!
> The courtier's, soldier's, scholar's eye, tongue, sword,
> Th'expectancy and rose of the fair state,
> The glass of fashion and the mould of form,
> Th'observed of all observers . . .

(III.1.151–155)

Hamlet's tragedy is that he ends by accepting the standards of behaviour his better nature rejects. At several points in the play we see him attempting to shed his moral sensitivity so as to take on the ruthless brutality of the avenger:

> Now could I drink hot blood
> And do such bitter business as the day
> Would quake to look on.
>
> (III.2.397–399)

> My thoughts be bloody, or be nothing worth!
>
> (IV.4.65–66)

By the final Act the transformation has taken place. Hamlet's cry when he interrupts Ophelia's funeral is peculiarly apposite in view of his submission to the values of Denmark:

> This is I,
> Hamlet the Dane.
>
> (V.1.253–254)

We learn that during the voyage to England he discovered Claudius's letter to the English king (ordering Hamlet's execution and replaced it with instructions that Rosencrantz and Guildenstern be put to death. This is an act that is Claudius-like in its cruelty (Hamlet stipulates that Rosencrantz and Guildenstern are to be allowed no time for confession before they die) and cunning. Hamlet feels no remorse: 'They are not near my conscience' (V.2.58).

An earlier indication of Hamlet's blunted sensitivity and moral judgement is his approval of Fortinbras's attack on Poland. Just before he leaves Denmark, Hamlet encounters Fortinbras's army as it passes through the outskirts of Elsinore (IV.4). A Captain tells him the purpose of the expedition is to gain an area of territory that is worth nothing to either side. Hamlet describes Fortinbras as 'a delicate and tender prince' and is impressed that he should lead his army into a battle where nothing but honour is at stake. He contrasts Fortinbras's determined pursuit of military success with his own failure to avenge his father's death:

> How all occasions do inform against me
> And spur my dull revenge!
>
> (IV.4.32–33)

He reproaches himself for his delay, whether it has been caused by 'craven scruple' or 'thinking too precisely on th'event'. At the close of the play, Fortinbras returns in triumph and Hamlet, before he dies, supports his election to the vacant Danish throne. But are we intended to applaud Fortinbras's accession and believe that it heralds the regeneration of Denmark? The answer has to be no. Fortinbras is unimpeded by 'craven scruple' and 'thinking too precisely on th'event' but it is exactly this that makes him a much lesser man than Hamlet. Shakespeare's account of the Polish expedition emphasises its futility, a futility that Hamlet, despite his apparent enthusiasm for the venture, clearly perceives. The Captain tells Hamlet:

> We go to gain a little patch of ground
> That hath in it no profit but the name.

> (IV.4.18–19)

And Hamlet is astonished that thousands of men are to 'debate the question of this straw'. In the closing speech of the scene, he has another damning metaphor for the object of this military contest, comparing it to an 'eggshell'. For Fortinbras, of course, the conflict is all about 'honour' rather than territorial acquisition. But this too is an illusory objective — a mere 'fantasy and trick of fame'. Fortinbras is said to be 'puffed' with 'ambition', and it is in the service of this vanity that 'twenty thousand men' face 'imminent death'. Fortinbras's shortcomings have in any case already been highlighted much earlier in the play. The account we were given of him in the opening scene suggested that he was impetuous and unprincipled: he had refused to accept the agreement made between his father and King Hamlet (a 'sealed compact,/ Well ratified by law and heraldry') and had 'Sharked up a list of lawless resolutes' to seize the lands his father lost to the Danish king.

It is difficult to view Fortinbras's accession as anything other than a triumph of mediocrity. He is, it is true, an effective man of action. He is also an outsider untainted by the corruption of the Danish court. But his coming to power does not mark a radical alteration in the ethos of Denmark; it remains a society in which the qualities we most admire in Hamlet have no place.

AFTERTHOUGHTS

1

Why does Gardiner use the word 'prison' at the end of the opening paragraph?

2

Do you agree with Gardiner's view of Laertes's character (pages 28–33) and of Fortinbras's character?

3

Do you agree that 'Hamlet is our guide to the world of the play and Shakespeare offers ample evidence to support his view of it' (page 31)?

4

Compare the account given here of Hamlet's behaviour in the final Act with Devlin's essay on pages 100–107.

Michael Gearin-Tosh

*Michael Gearin-Tosh is Fellow and
Tutor in English Literature at St
Catherine's College, Oxford. He is also
Associate Director of the Oxford School
of Drama.*

ESSAY

The significance of Hamlet's second soliloquy (II.2.546–603)

In his opening scenes, Shakespeare often suggests how behaviour should be valued. The suggestions are oblique and not
didactic: they subtly announce or hint at themes which the
action of the play will explore. In *Hamlet* the description of
Fortinbras is extraneous to the immediate events of the first
scene, as is the description of Christmas. The ideas behind these
descriptions establish a counterpoint which resonates throughout
the play.

Horatio describes Fortinbras's character at I.1.95–100:

> Now, sir, young Fortinbras,
> Of unimprovèd mettle hot and full,
> Hath in the skirts of Norway here and there
> Sharked up a list of lawless resolutes
> For food and diet to some enterprise
> That hath a stomach in't . . .

'Sharked up' is scathing: 'snatching up indiscriminately as a
shark does its food' is the gloss of the Arden editor. This lack

of discrimination is also the point of 'unimproved'. Fortinbras
has not developed his character; he has crude, animal 'mettle'.

Christmas is the subject of Marcellus's speech when the
Ghost leaves:

> It faded on the crowing of the cock.
> Some say that ever 'gainst that season comes
> Wherein our Saviour's birth is celebrated,
> This bird of dawning singeth all night long.
> And then, they say, no spirit dare stir abroad;
> The nights are wholesome; then no planets strike;
> No fairy takes; nor witch hath power to charm.
> So hallowed and so gracious is that time.

> (I.1.158–165)

No other tragedy by Shakespeare opens with so overt a reference
to Christ. This celebration of providence is also enacted by the
movement of the scene, which starts with frightened parleys by
night and the terror of the Ghost. But after Marcellus's speech,
light floods in:

> But look, the morn in russet mantle clad
> Walks o'er the dew of yon high eastward hill.

> (I.1.167–168)

This personification is not merely decorative: it suggests a presence in the universe which brings light after darkness.

The descriptions of Fortinbras and of Christmas are complementary in that no Christian may be 'unimproved'. The life of
spiritual discipline and grace is concerned to achieve what
Fortinbras ignores, a growing habit of religious observance, love
and charity:

> ... make the tree good, and his fruit good ... A good man out
> of the good treasure of the heart bringeth forth good things: and
> an evil man out of the evil treasure bringeth forth evil things.

> (Matthew 12:33, 35 — Authorised Version)

> Purge out therefore the old leaven, that ye may be a new lump
> ...

> (I Corinthians 5:7 — Authorised Version)

> ... leaving your former way of life, you must lay aside that old

human nature which, deluded by its lusts, is sinking towards death. You must be made new in mind and spirit . . .

(Ephesians 4:22–23 — New English Bible)

Fortinbras serves as a foil to Hamlet's spiritual growth.

Two seminal critics, Coleridge and Schlegel, write as if Hamlet had no effective faith, yet his first soliloquy begins by observing that the Commandment 'Thou shalt not kill' forbade suicide as well as murder according to contemporary interpretation:

> O that this too too sullied flesh would melt,
> Thaw, and resolve itself into a dew;
> Or that the Everlasting had not fixed
> His canon 'gainst self-slaughter. O God, God
>
> (I.2.129–132)

Shakespeare gives Hamlet the habit of thinking in religious terms: 'For God's love, let me hear!' (I.2.195); 'I'll speak to it though hell itself should gape/ And bid me hold my peace' (I.2.245–246); 'Angels and ministers of grace defend us!' (I.4.39); and when Horatio and Marcellus try to dissuade him from following the Ghost:

> Why, what should be the fear?
> I do not set my life at a pin's fee,
> And for my soul, what can it do to that,
> Being a thing immortal as itself?
>
> (I.4.64–67)

Schlegel saw Hamlet's faith as superficial and inconstant:

> Hamlet is a hypocrite towards himself: his far-fetched scruples are often mere pretexts to cover his want of determination; thoughts, as he says on a different occasion, which have
> > but one part wisdom
> > And ever three parts coward.
>
> Hamlet has no firm belief either in himself or in anything else: from expressions of religious confidence he passes over to sceptical doubts; he believes in the Ghost of his father when he sees it, and as soon as it has disappeared, it appears to him almost in light of a deception.

Coleridge found that Hamlet suffers from 'meditative excess' with 'a consequent proportionate aversion to real action'. It is hard to be certain of what Coleridge thought because his influential lectures on Hamlet are not extant. Some jottings and rough notes survive, but our only sustained account is in another man's words: a young admirer, J P Collier, attended his lecture of 1811 and took notes which he published some forty-five years later. He gave Coleridge's conclusion as:

> Hamlet is a man living in meditation, called upon to act by every motive human and divine, but the great object of his life is defeated by continually resolving to do, yet doing nothing but resolve.

This is a questionable use of 'divine' and I shall try to show that it flaws the argument.

Although Hamlet's soliloquies exceed those of any other tragic hero in Shakespeare, we have to wait more than 650 lines before the second soliloquy shows us Hamlet's reactions to the Ghost. This is an extraordinary postponement and the soliloquy, when it comes, is remarkable. It is the longest soliloquy in Shakespeare's plays apart from Richard II's:

> I have been studying how I may compare
> This prison where I live unto the world.

> (V.5.1–2)

Yet where Richard attempts to construct something in the isolation of prison, Hamlet's soliloquy is spoken in the midst of bustling action. Richard's soliloquy is the climax of the play, delivered just before his murder: in *Hamlet*, Shakespeare takes the risk of stilling the action for sixty lines before the third Act has even started. Music plays during the last third of Richard's speech and gives variety. There is no such relief in Hamlet's soliloquy: we are made to concentrate exclusively on his mind.

The soliloquy is delayed because Shakespeare shows not an immediate, shocked reaction to the Ghost, but how Hamlet has begun to absorb the terror and challenge. The focus is upon these deeper processes whose shape and potential form his character.

The soliloquy begins as a reaction to the Players, who arrived a hundred lines earlier. Hamlet had asked them for a speech, not any speech but one that he 'chiefly loved' (II.2.444): he promptly remembered and quoted the first thirteen lines. The play has not prepared us for a Hamlet who loves lines which are crudely horrific:

> 'The rugged Pyrrhus, he whose sable arms,
> Black as his purpose, did the night resemble
> When he lay couchèd in th'ominous horse,
> Hath now this dread and black complexion smeared
> With heraldry more dismal. Head to foot
> Now is he total gules, horridly tricked
> With blood of fathers, mothers, daughters, sons,
> Baked and impasted with the parching streets,
> That lend a tyrannous and a damnèd light
> To their lord's murder; roasted in wrath and fire,
> And thus o'er-sizèd with coagulate gore,
> With eyes like carbuncles, the hellish Pyrrhus
> Old grandsire Priam seeks.'

(II.2.450–462)

This incident, as Hamlet told the actor, comes from 'Aeneas' tale to Dido' (II.2.445) about the fall of Troy and the killing of King Priam by the Greeks:

> Priam, trembling, and slipping in the blood which flowed from his son's corpse, was dragged to the altar by Pyrrhus, who twisted Priam's hair in his left hand, and drawing his flashing sword with his right, plunged it to the hilt in Priam's side.

(Virgil, *Aeneid* 2.550–554)

The horror in Virgil's account comes from Priam being killed in the gore of his own dead son. Shakespeare leaves this out and instead gives a description of Pyrrhus. The only visual detail in Virgil is that Pyrrhus wore shining brass armour (*Aeneid* 2.470). Shakespeare dresses him in black armour (lines 450–451) which is 'smeared' with blood at line 453 and, two lines later, he is red all over: 'Now is he total gules'. This blood is then baked into a crust (line 457) by the heat of Troy which is now on fire. Shakespeare then observes — it is characteristic of his concentration and sensuousness that he should add this detail to his source — that armour in a blazing city must become torturingly hot to wear: Pyrrhus is 'roasted in wrath and fire' (line 459) beneath his crust of clotted blood, 'o'er-sizèd with coagulate gore' (line 460).

In the soliloquy, Hamlet begins by rebuking himself for lacking the passion of the actor who finished the speech about Pyrrhus:

> What would he do
> Had he the motive and the cue for passion
> That I have? He would drown the stage with tears
> And cleave the general ear with horrid speech
>
> (II.2.557–560)

It is understandable that Hamlet should ask this question, but can speech be more 'horrid' than the ghoulish account of Pyrrhus which Hamlet himself has just given? The account would seem especially bizarre to Elizabethans who knew Virgil well and would be alert to how he had been changed.

The shock of meeting the Ghost has led Hamlet to mark time: he instinctively thinks of literature and uses it. Although there was a very general resemblance between Priam and his own father, what matters is that he has chosen a lurid treatment because its sensationalism suits his shock and rage. In the soliloquy, the Pyrrhus lines serve as a model which he now imitates, and the artistic logic of making the soliloquy a response to the players is to enforce this theme of derivativeness. Hamlet behaves like a character in a play — one of the revenge plays which were popular at the time and whose heroes fulminate in a mode of 'horrid speech' which comes from Marlowe. Indeed, the Pyrrhus speech may allude to this influence by recalling Marlowe's first play *Dido, Queen of Carthage*:

> At last came Pyrrhus, fell and full of ire,
> His harnessing dropping blood, and on his spear
> The mangled head of Priam's youngest son . . .
> And after him his band of Myrmidons
> With balls of wild fire in their murdering paws
>
> (II.1.213–217)

Shakespeare had written a revenge play some seven years before *Hamlet*. In *Titus Andronicus*, the deeds are so horrid that some muting of 'horrid speech' is possible, but it exerts an influence. In the last Act, Titus makes an empress eat her own sons in a pastry. Just before he slits their throats, he declares:

> Hark, villains, I will grind your bones to dust,
> And with your blood and it I'll make a paste
> . . .
> And make two pasties of your shameful heads
> And bid that strumpet, your unhallowed dam,
> Like to the earth swallow her own increase.

(V.2.186–192)

We hear similar tones from Hamlet — if he were not a coward, he would have killed Claudius by now:

> . . . ere this
> I should ha' fatted all the region kites
> With this slave's offal.

(II.2.575–577)

This is wildly remote from the world of *Hamlet*. It is in ancient Greek tragedy that corpses are left for the birds, and even there it is denounced as barbarous. Titus would have intended literally to plump 'the region kites', but Hamlet soon sees these lines as an indulgence. In doing so, he denies by implication the assumption of minor revenge plays that 'horrid speech' stimulates action.

The breakthrough occurs in lines 580–586 where Hamlet turns on himself with:

> Why, what an ass am I! This is most brave,
> That I, the son of a dear father murdered,
> Prompted to my revenge by heaven and hell,
> Must like a whore unpack my heart with words
> And fall a-cursing like a very drab

This is fierce self-criticism and its vehemence is matched by its acuteness. Hamlet 'chiefly loved' the lines on Pyrrhus and in doing so he was 'like a whore' in the sense that the lines were action without soul: Pyrrhus is not only destined to kill Priam, he must be gruesomely decked for the part and driven to a pitch of physical discomfort to match his fury. These intensifications are what fantasy craves when it becomes a substitute for the life of the heart.

By rejecting 'horrid speech', Hamlet is 'purging out the old leaven' and when his 'brains' take over, we hear a different voice:

> . . . I have heard
> That guilty creatures sitting at a play
> Have by the very cunning of the scene
> Been struck so to the soul that presently
> They have proclaimed their malefactions.
> For murder, though it have no tongue, will speak
> With most miraculous organ. I'll have these players
> Play something like the murder of my father
> Before mine uncle. I'll observe his looks.
> I'll tent him to the quick. If 'a do blench,
> I know my course.
>
> (II.2.586–596)

In these lucid and unornamented lines, 'miraculous' is given much emphasis. It refers to the supernatural, as does 'organ', which, in addition to its anatomical sense, was used of the instrument by which a supernatural purpose is executed. Thus in *All's Well That Ends Well* the King tells Helen, when he believes she may cure him:

> Methinks in thee some blessed spirit doth speak
> His powerful sound within an organ weak;
> And what impossibility would slay
> In common sense, sense saves another way,
>
> (II.1.175–178)

It is by divine power that Hamlet's murderer is forced to confess, the divine power which loosens the tongues of the dumb in miracles. 'Horrid speech' is replaced by a plan which is conceived in the context of faith.

When Schlegel argued that Hamlet passes from 'religious confidence' to 'sceptical doubts', the evidence was that Hamlet believes in the Ghost when he sees it, but then views it 'almost in the light of a deception'. This occurs at the end of the second soliloquy. Although Hamlet declared at line 582 that he was 'Prompted to my revenge by heaven and hell', now he is not so sure:

> The spirit that I have seen
> May be a devil, and the devil hath power
> T'assume a pleasing shape, yea, and perhaps
> Out of my weakness and my melancholy,
> As he is very potent with such spirits,
> Abuses me to damn me.

(II.2.596–601)

In one of his jottings, Coleridge noted against these lines:

> See Sir Thomas Browne: Those apparitions and ghosts of departed persons are not the wandering souls of men, but the unquiet walks of devils, prompting and suggesting us unto mischief, blood and villainy.

Browne's *Religio Medici* was written in the mid-1630s and published in 1642. Writing before *Hamlet*, Nashe noted specifically that it was in the form of a dead father that the devil could incite to evil:

> It will bee demaunded why in the likenes of ones father or mother, or kinsfolke, he oftentimes presents himselfe unto us?
>
> No other reason can bee given of it but this, that in those shapes which hee supposeth most familliar unto us, and that wee are inclined to with a naturall kind of love, we will sooner harken to him than otherwise.

(*The Terrors of the Night* — 1594)

Hamlet's doubts are not 'far-fetched scruples' as Schlegel wrote: they were natural to a man of faith. Nor is it easy to believe that Coleridge, if he had thought of Browne at the time of the 1811 lecture, would argue that Hamlet was 'called upon to act by every motive human and divine'.

Hamlet's plan is resourceful. The Ghost ordered him to:

> Revenge his foul and most unnatural murder.

(I.5.25)

But revenge is forbidden to Christians (Deuteronomy 32:35, cited in Romans 12:19). Yet there were those who considered regicide a grave sin, even a blasphemy: what if assassination was the only way of punishing it in practice? This was a spiritual quicksand. Hamlet's first priority was to be sure of Claudius's guilt, if possible doubly sure. The Players arrived unexpectedly yet after 130 lines Hamlet had the idea of *The Murder of Gonzago* with his insertion (II.2.534–539). And his plan went further. He tells us in the second soliloquy that murderers have 'proclaimed their malefactions'. 'Proclaim' means to state publicly. If this happened, we assume Claudius would be dethroned and the Commandment against murder would not be broken. Coleridge attacked Hamlet for a lack of 'real action', but 'real action' for a Christian is acting by the standards of faith and in this sense Hamlet deserves praise.

Titus Andronicus and *Hamlet* end with the hero killing his persecutor who, in both cases, 'is justly served' as Laertes exclaims at Claudius's death (V.2.321). Titus kills Tamora with a savage and calculated vengeance, but Claudius is killed almost on the spur of the moment when events expose him as a man of multiple evil. The last Act of *Titus Andronicus* focuses on Titus's plans. But Hamlet does not plot against Claudius after the voyage to England: Claudius and Laertes plot against him. Our interest has passed beyond Hamlet's motive into his attitudes, and this is one reason why *Hamlet* is a very great play and *Titus Andronicus* is not.

Hamlet makes an important advance upon the attitude to providence which he holds at the end of the second soliloquy. It is dangerous for a Christian to rely on a specific miracle because that may conflict with the great prayer to God: 'Thy will be done'. Before the final duel, Hamlet tells Horatio 'how ill all's here about my heart' (V.2.206–207). Horatio urges him to withdraw, but Hamlet refuses:

> Not a whit. We defy augury. There is special providence in the fall of a sparrow. If it be now, 'tis not to come. If it be not to come, it will be now. If it be not now, yet it will come. The readiness is all. Since no man knows of aught he leaves, what is't to leave betimes? Let be.

> (V.2.213–218)

Hamlet's comment on 'special providence' alludes directly and closely to Matthew 10:28–31:

> And fear not them which kill the body, but are not able to kill the soul: but rather fear him which is able to destroy both soul

and body in hell.

> Are not two sparrows sold for a farthing? And one of them shall not fall on the ground without your Father.
>
> But the very hairs of your head are all numbered.
>
> Fear ye not therefore, ye are of more value than many sparrows.

This is our final insight into Hamlet's mind before the duel. Psychologically he is strong enough to go forward even when his self-protective instincts urge him to withdraw. The allusion to St Matthew makes it clear that his faith is a source of this strength. He has achieved the rare distinction of being open to providence and trusting it. This challenges Schlegel's argument that 'Hamlet has no firm belief either in himself or in anything else'.

Hamlet also differs from *Titus Andronicus* in the range of the last three Acts. Both plays are increasingly concerned with the hero's state of mind, but where we spend more and more time with Titus in 'his woeful house' (V.2.82), in *Hamlet* the former relisher of 'horrid speech' lectures the actors on not tearing 'a passion to tatters' (III.2.9–10), flirts with Ophelia, gives Rosencrantz and Guildenstern their verbal and later physical come-uppance, encounters Claudius and Gertrude, kills Polonius, watches Fortinbras's army and sets sail for England. Also, we see the Players' dumb show and hear the play; there is the scene with Ophelia; Claudius plots with Laertes; we meet the gravediggers. *Titus Andronicus* becomes claustrophobic; *Hamlet* has the breadth of Fielding and Dickens.

This breadth is the artistic corollary of Hamlet's inner expansion. Titus narrows his vision to focus on revenge and nothing else; he urges his family to:

> . . . eat no more
> Than will preserve just so much strength in us
> As will revenge these bitter woes of ours.

> (III.2.1–3)

Hamlet's speculative temperament had always enjoyed the frontiers of experience: we feel it was from the heart that he urged Horatio to welcome the Ghost 'as a stranger' (1.5.165) and he revels in his bizarre but truthful gibes about Polonius:

> A man may fish with the worm that hath eat of a king, and eat
> of the fish that hath fed of that worm.
>
> (IV.3.26–27)

But he grows in the ability to confront others and himself nearer home. He is scarcely judicious. But he is courageous and warm with Gertrude, and he is generous about Fortinbras who is not 'a delicate and tender prince' (IV.4.48). Hamlet is able to declare his love for Ophelia even if too late and in a quarrel which is ridiculous but full of pathos.

People do not grow without relapses. None of Hamlet's relapses is more embarrassing in spiritual terms than his lines when he finds Claudius praying (III.3.73–96): Dr Johnson called them 'too horrible to be read or to be uttered', and in Christian terms they are little less than a denial of Christianity. But it should be noted that they are a relapse. Hamlet fulminates as he did in the early part of the second soliloquy:

> Then trip him, that his heels may kick at heaven,
> And that his soul may be as damned and black
> As hell, whereto it goes.
>
> (III.3.93–95)

Shakespeare calls attention to this idiom when Hamlet uses the word 'horrid' in line 88:

> Up, sword, and know thou a more horrid hent.

'Horrid speech' is a type of literary self-stupefaction. Its obverse, for Hamlet, is mimicry, and an index of the buoyancy of his spirit is the gusto with which he satirises the engulfing humbug of Elsinore. In the last scene, he tells Horatio about his pastiche of Claudius in the letter to England:

> As England was his faithful tributary,
> As love between them like the palm might flourish,
> As peace should still her wheaten garland wear
> And stand a comma 'tween their amities,
> And many such-like as's of great charge
>
> (V.2.39–43)

It is most apt to move from citing the Psalms in line 40 to punning on asses in line 43. Osric is then served up as a victim with the *coup de grâce*:

The concernancy, sir? Why do we wrap the gentleman in our more rawer breath?

(V.2.121–122)

A result of the play's breadth is the paradox that we know more of Hamlet by being apart from him. Titus Andronicus has a less rich character, but it is also true that, in Blake's words, the play:

... examines every little fibre of his soul,
Spreading them out before the sun like stalks of flax to dry.

(*Vala* 1, 39–40)

But with Hamlet, we move between surprise as we learn more about the range of his character, and delight at discovering his coherences, which are not obvious or so all-embracing that his psychology is schematic. It is shortly after the second soliloquy that Hamlet gives his lethal rebuke to Rosencrantz and Guildenstern:

Why, look you now, how unworthy a thing you make of me! You would play upon me. You would seem to know my stops. You would pluck out the heart of my mystery.... 'Sblood, do you think I am easier to be played on than a pipe?

(III.2.371–378)

The lines are also a warning to critics. Shakespeare's great characters keep their power to surprise us and also themselves, and this is as clearly enacted in Hamlet's second soliloquy as anywhere. It gives a rare insight into the dynamics of a hero's mind, Hamlet's instinctive alliance with what is most alive in himself, his courage to reject what will not do and to create almost from nothing a new way of going forward. Such creation is at odds with being 'unimproved', as Horatio described Fortinbras, and in Hamlet's case both his initial way forward and its subsequent redirections are in accord with his faith.

This may be why Shakespeare gives Hamlet the unique distinction of two valedictions. Fortinbras delivers the formal farewell:

Let four captains
Bear Hamlet like a soldier to the stage.

(V.2.389–390)

But Christians are also soldiers in another sense:

> Wherefore take unto you the whole armour of God, that ye may be able to withstand in the evil day, and having done all, to stand. . . .
> Above all, taking the shield of faith, wherewith ye shall be able to quench all the fiery darts of the wicked.
>
> (Ephesians 6:13,16)

In this warfare it is 'the shield of faith' which is used rather than the soldier's sword. Thus it is appropriate that Hamlet's dear friend Horatio should also bid Hamlet adieu:

> Now cracks a noble heart. Good night, sweet Prince,
> And flights of angels sing thee to thy rest!
>
> (V.2.353–354)

One of Coleridge's notes is more sympathetic to Hamlet than the others, at least potentially. Commenting on 'To be, or not to be . . .' (III.1.56–88), he wrote:

> Of such universal interest, and yet to which of all Shakespeare's characters could it have been *appropriately* given but to Hamlet? For Jaques it would have been too deep; for Iago, too habitual a communion with the *heart*, that belongs, or ought to belong, to all mankind.

'Habitual communion with the heart' is the essence of an integrity which is not static or bound to rules but living, open and therefore liable to change, to expansion and not caprice. It is a force which transcends the hypocrisy which Schlegel alleged. Rosencrantz and Guildenstern are hypocrites whom we cannot imagine conducting a genuine dialogue of thought and feeling. Claudius at least can. He knows he is a hypocrite and that makes him a villain. Hamlet not only consults his heart, he has the habit of doing so. Habits of this kind require self-discipline and courage, two of the qualities which make Hamlet a hero. Both qualities are shown in operation during the second soliloquy.

AFTERTHOUGHTS

1

What significance does Gearin-Tosh attach to the reference to Christmas at I.1.160? How does this inform the argument of his essay as a whole?

2

How helpful do you find it to refer to the opinions of 'seminal critics' (page 37)?

3

What do you think Gearin-Tosh has in mind when he states that Hamlet has 'achieved the rare distinction of being open to providence and trusting it' (page 45)?

4

In what ways does Gearin-Tosh relates analysis of an individual speech to the concerns of the play as a whole.

Stephen Siddall

Stephen Siddall is Head of English at the Leys School, Cambridge.

ESSAY

Hamlet and the Player King's speech

Hamlet contains three major court scenes, positioned symmetrically at the beginning, middle and end of the play. Each is very self-consciously staged to conceal the deviousness of its manager. The first and third are arranged by Claudius, and they act as glittering frames for the spread action of the play which is often domestic and always tangled. The public nature of both is designed to enclose the private actions and thoughts of an erratic hero, and their positioning at the beginning and end of the tragedy gives added force to Hamlet's view that 'Denmark's a prison'. At the opening court scene the King presides and proclaims his obviously prepared mixture of domestic benevolence and firm foreign policy, with himself as leading player and Laertes and Polonius as cooperative 'bit-part' actors. It is only Hamlet who rejects his required role and, with equal self-consciousness, adopts his own — that of black-clad malcontent. In Act V, Claudius is again the entrepreneur, but this time Laertes and Hamlet, as duellists, are the cooperative central performers as they play out a hostility that the King has manipulated, and in part created. The dramatic tension of Act I was based on the fact that both young men found Elsinore oppressive and wanted to escape; now, in their different ways they have been drawn back to 'prison' to become instruments in the King's final act of stage-management.

Laertes's escape has lasted for three Acts, whereas Hamlet's brief period of freedom has been no more than an episode in the tangle of Act IV. However, being a more complex character than Laertes, he finds the pressures on him more varied and destructive — hence his need for release is greater. Hamlet's frustration dominates Acts II and III. He searches for emotional outlets in ways that almost invariably hurt himself and other people. Sometimes he indulges in strangely alienating behaviour, as with Ophelia in her closet; sometimes his attack is through the railing and sarcasm of his superior intellect. Whatever the method, and however misguided, his aim is freedom, and when speaking with Rosencrantz and Guildenstern he explains the difference between physical and emotional freedom:

> O God, I could be bounded in a nutshell and count myself a king of infinite space, were it not that I have bad dreams.
>
> (II.2.253–255)

At this point in the play, the arrival of his friends may have seemed to him like a diversion from the oppressive Elsinore and a way for him to tap the energy and freedom of university life. But any sense of release is soon thwarted when he recognises them as manipulators and agents. In response they are embarrassed and react with feeble superficiality of wit. It is perhaps ironic that the 'substance' of their talk is about 'shadows and dreams', so floating the idea of a world other than this one in which Hamlet might lose himself. Immediately Polonius introduces the Players, who, in common Elizabethan metaphor, could be described as the 'shadows' of real people. Their profession is to enact dreams and fantasies, and Hamlet welcomes them with more genuine enthusiasm than he shows at any other time in the play.

It is not difficult to see why Hamlet values the theatre and the Players. As a rebel and idealist, he himself constantly adopts roles in relation to the world he inhabits, generally to disconcert the orthodox: Gertrude, Claudius, Polonius, Ophelia (and later Osric and Laertes) all have to face performances from him that are designed to baffle and humiliate. But beyond these there is the role of revenge hero which presents him and the audience with such perplexing ambivalence. He castigates himself for being too frail to take on the role; he also questions both its moral validity and the honesty of the Ghost that has invited him to play the part.

For Hamlet, then, there is some relief in escaping from the problems of his 'real-life' role and into the work of classical fiction where emotions are large-scale and duties clear-cut. The story of Pyrrhus, Priam and Hecuba is simple and strong, whilst the Players who perform it are rootless Elizabethan wanderers, living outside social norms with nothing expected of them personally beyond the acquired skills to present the massive personalities of fiction. Hamlet's own life is the opposite: his own thoughts and emotions tangle frustratingly, whilst his social position brings with it expectations which are precise and therefore imprisoning. He envies the Players' freedom both in physical travel and mobile identity. He enters their world, firstly as informal patron and audience at a set-piece 'purple passage', then as a drama-school instructor, then as a playwright and finally (in performance) as entrepreneur and intrusive commentator.

At the welcoming ceremony Hamlet had asked his old friend, the heroic actor, to 'study a speech of some dozen or sixteen lines' which could be inserted into the story of *The Murder of Gonzago* without, presumably, affecting the plot. That speech is never identified — it may be that the Players had not reached it when the King abandoned the entertainment. It may have been a speech that drew *The Murder of Gonzago* even closer to the story of old King Hamlet, Gertrude and Claudius, or it may have been one that reflected Hamlet's thoughts moving away from such specific concerns and into more general observations about trust, idealism and inconstancy. In this last case it could have been the long speech which begins with the words, 'I do believe you think what now you speak' (III.2.196), in which the Player King lectures his rather naïve queen. It is only of marginal interest, though, to identify this as Hamlet's contribution; what is much more significant is that the speech stands at the very centre of Shakespeare's play, that it is framed within the great central court scene, and that its language and thought bear on Hamlet's predicament in ways that are not found elsewhere in the play.

The Player Queen has just sworn eternal fidelity to her husband, not, we feel, because she is being presented as a steady and decisive person, but because her nerviness makes her wish for these qualities. Like Hamlet after hearing the Player's heroic demonstration speech, she behaves as though a flood of words, laced with hyperbole and repetition, might urge her into the integrity she wants to possess. However, in reply, the Player King acknowledges and accepts human frailty; the maturity expressed in his lines is that we should not expect too much of ourselves nor rail savagely against others who fail to live up to the highest ideals:

> Most necessary 'tis that we forget
> To pay ourselves what to ourselves is debt.

(III.2.202–203)

The contrast between their two points of view comes close to Hamlet's own predicament. How can an idealist — filled with the talents which Ophelia described in her eulogy of him — accommodate himself to disappointment? It is a commonplace that the most bitter cynic is likely to be the man who was once the most glowing idealist. For Hamlet, the world (as expressed in the court) has proved corrupt and the people close to him unreliable. His response has been to attack and disconcert them — and, at times, to attack himself for such futile behaviour. The Player King's speech presents an alternative and more mature course, which, even though Hamlet may have written it into the play, he still cannot embody in his own behaviour. Indeed, it may be that to tackle the problem in fiction and express it in the theatre is a sensible way to work on himself vicariously. If so, the play becomes the thing partly to 'catch the conscience of the King' (II.2.602–603), and partly too to touch the conscience of the prince-playwright. We know that Hamlet has this problem in the forefront of his mind; shortly before the perform-ance begins he praises Horatio for not being 'passion's slave' (III.2.82) and for having (like the Player King) only moderate expectations of life and other people.

To accept one's frailty — like submitting to the vagaries of fortune — is particularly difficult for people of high rank, from whom important decisions are constantly expected. *The Murder of Gonzago* is about kings and queens; so is the story of Hamlet and Claudius. Men of heroic (or at least public) status are expected to influence the course of events, especially when they are:

> Th'expectancy and rose of the fair state,
> The glass of fashion and the mould of form,
> Th'observed of all observers . . .

> (III.1.153–155)

It is with this in mind that Hamlet may struggle to receive his own advice when the Player King comes near to patronising his queen in the words:

> I do believe you think what now you speak,
> But what we do determine oft we break.

> (III.2.196–197)

The humiliating truth is explained further in the two lines that follow:

> Purpose is but the slave to memory,
> Of violent birth, but poor validity,

and then neatly summarised at the end of the speech:

> Our thoughts are ours, their ends none of our own.

> (III.2.223)

So the most we can hope for is that there be integrity in our initial impulse; for the Player Queen this refers to her wish to be loyal beyond her husband's death, and for Hamlet it might refer to his revenge 'duty', though in such a questioning play both he and Shakespeare throw considerable doubt on whether or not the duty is valid, just as he is — here — doubting an individual's capacity to sustain commitment. The more violent the birth of such impulse, the more humiliating for an over-scrupulous idealist when:

> . . . the native hue of resolution
> Is sicklied o'er with the pale cast of thought

> (III.1.84–85)

Apart from these worries about the hero's resolve, there are external circumstances — also unpredictable. The ends of our thoughts are 'none of our own', not just through internal frailty (or 'poor validity'), but because we are influenced by events and people outside ourselves. We live in the mortal world in which, predictably, time passes, but in which (unpredictably) events are random and so the circumstances we face are muddled. To cope with this the Player King speaks of compromise. In doing so, he hopes to make his queen see that maturity lies in our being able to judge wisely how an absolute principle can adapt to the cross-currents that time brings with it. Ideally it should be possible to colour (if not, quite, to alter) one's firm values without having to lose self-respect or be a feather for each wind that blows.

However, as the speech continues, it becomes hard to see the Player King sustaining this middle way. We may even begin to feel that he is creating a philosophy that justifies the instinctive pragmatism of a Polonius or Osric. ''Tis not strange', he says, 'That even our loves should with our fortunes change' (III.2.210–211). He then illustrates the point with a survey of a world in which everyone observes a great man's fortunes and follows him on his upward path. It would be typical of Hamlet's restless temperament to drive the speech to this worrying extreme, so that he can find every course of action and every philosophy of life to be untenable. What here begins as a salutary check to the Player Queen's excessive idealism becomes a melancholy observation on the way things are. The last lines of his play-life seem to tilt more towards tiredness and gloom than to a settled wisdom. His 'spirits grow dull', he wants to be left alone and to end his 'tedious day' (and life) with sleep. Then enters the man of action, Lucianus, who, as nephew to the King, is Hamlet in another role — that of the avenger:

> Thoughts black, hands apt, drugs fit, and time agreeing.
>
> (III.2.264)

This violent language leaves no room for Hamlet's own 'real-life' questioning. Perhaps such decisiveness really is the healthier course? At times, as in the moment just before he visits his mother, he comes close to adopting it. And when, in Act V, he sees Laertes uncomplicatedly pursuing his aim without finding that his 'Purpose is but the slave to memory' (III.2.198), then Hamlet is torn between envy and contempt for him. Throughout the play, Hamlet is a restless experimenter with different approaches to his problems, and through *The Murder of Gonzago* he not only proposes one of them, but drives it to a point where it can't be accepted.

At the centre of this central speech in the play lies the melancholy truth that 'This world is not for aye' (III.2.210). The whole philosophy of changing circumstances, as well as the fickleness of human emotions ('Grief joys, joy grieves on slender accident'), hangs on this simple statement. Great purposes, ambitions, human energies and convulsions in the state appear trivial when placed in the context of this truth. And it is a tension often to be found in tragedy that a hero aware of the power within him and his faculties stretched to their extreme, is also aware that his significance in the span of human history is minimal. Macbeth recognises it in Act V when he compares himself to the 'poor player', a mere 'shadow' whose out-poured energy is so futile. Like Hamlet's, Macbeth's behaviour is erratic and disconcerting, but Hamlet's bitterness is less sustained and his responses to the light fading are influenced by more searching thoughts. In his Act V the recognition that life is temporary appears in more varied incidents: his finding Yorick's skull, Ophelia's death and burial, and then, just before the court bears down on him for the final duel, his quiet discussion with Horatio about submission:

> Since no man knows of aught he leaves, what is't to leave betimes? Let be.

> (V.2.216–218)

At this point the tone of the hero's philosophy is slightly different from that of the fictional Player King. It is a difference between gloom and sober acceptance. And both the stage pictures and the subsequent events are different for the two episodes. The Player King lies down and sleeps into his murder. Hamlet's end is public: an isolated, vulnerable figure waits for the court and the King's purposes to surround him, he engages in traditional courtesies (though tinged with irony at Laertes's expense), he performs with grace, reacts with outrage at treachery, and dies with the gentler virtues of forgiveness and concern for reputation, which is the only way in which a young hero can challenge the truth of 'This world is not for aye'.

Towards its end, the Player King's speech moves from philosophy for an individual and into social commentary.

This section begins with a disingenuous pretence at fair objectivity:

> For 'tis a question left us yet to prove,
> Whether love lead fortune, or else fortune love.
>
> (III.2.212–213)

But the real point of the speech is not to leave the question open for doubt: the certain answer is that fortune leads love — i.e. that the circumstances we meet condition our emotional and moral responses. The Player King draws his evidence from the court (as Hamlet himself would), because the extremes of 'Fortune's buffets and rewards' are more vivid there and the dangers are greater. In *King Lear*, commenting on the ways of this world, the Fool advises prudence to Kent. In similar terms here the Player King says:

> The great man down, you mark his favourite flies.
> The poor advanced makes friends of enemies.
>
> (III.2.214–215)

Outside this performance, Hamlet has observed how easily allegiances change from one regime to another, how his mother adapts flexibly from one marriage to another, and how Rosencrantz and Guildenstern (and even Ophelia, in his view) are prepared to become instruments in furtive purposes. Politics, whether in the state or the family, may be defined as the art of making smooth and convenient what has been decreed. Such hypocrisy disgusts Hamlet, whereas the Player King presents it ruefully as a condition of real life. In fact, he takes it a stage further by intimating that the hypocrites retain enough moral awareness to feel uncomfortable when their flexibility is brought into the open; rather than react with *self*-criticism, their instinct instead is to resent the petitioner who raised the problem:

> For who not needs shall never lack a friend,
> And who in want a hollow friend doth try
> Directly seasons him his enemy.
>
> (III.3.217–219)

This is the most cynical point of the speech, and the Player King takes the argument no further, whereas Hamlet, if reacting in his own life to specific circumstances of this nature, would have been more sharp, intense and violent. Instead, the speech announces its intention to be shapely rather than direct; the Player King indicates the pattern of his sermon and returns to the start:

> But, orderly to end where I begun,
> Our wills and fates do so contrary run
> That our devices still are overthrown.
> Our thoughts are ours, their ends none of our own.
>
> (III.2.220–223)

He then follows this generalised reminder about the vanity of human wishes by returning to his cue from the story of the play:

> So think thou wilt no second husband wed,
> But die thy thoughts when thy first lord is dead.
>
> (III.2.224–225)

The orderly and distanced nature of the speech as a whole turns it into a brief moral capsule set in the very centre of the story of *Hamlet*, which itself is framed by the two outer court scenes. The speech comes in the middle of the central court scene, similar to the other two in that it is a calculated performance, but different in that Hamlet, not Claudius, is the manipulator. Its rhyming couplets distance it from the rest of the play, giving it a control and generalised quality quite unlike the emotions felt by the main characters. It feels not unlike some moral verse epistles written in the eighteenth century: control and clarity are the marks of civilised man, and there is a slightly chill dignity in applying these virtues to the most troubling problems that people have to face. Since the themes and concerns of the speech are close to Hamlet's own, it may begin to feel like a type of wish-fulfilment. In his own life Hamlet cannot achieve order or detached reflection — hence his admiration for Horatio — but through art he can reach the impossible and hold a moment of truth. The speech, then, has the advantages firstly of its distanced style and secondly of its position in the play, framed by (and within) the court scenes and so layered back as far as possible from the play's real action. This is a technique used strikingly by Shakespeare in other plays (*The Tempest* and *The Winter's Tale* are notable examples). The manipulator — in this case Hamlet — establishes a play within the play in order to experiment with ideas that are too close to be tackled steadily in his own life. This 'escapism', if we can call it that, is potentially enriching and clarifying — for the audience as well as for Hamlet. As Martin Esslin has put it in his studies in modern drama, the theatre may be seen as a laboratory in which approaches to life may be tried out with minimum danger and, as here, with the advantage of focus and shape that a more formal language can give.

AFTERTHOUGHTS

1

What are the 'three major court scenes' referred to in the opening sentence of this essay?

2

. What do you understand by Hamlet's 'real-life' role (page 52)? How important is role-play to *Hamlet* as a whole?

3

In what ways does the play-within-a-play draw attention to Hamlet's concern with theatricality?

4

What arguments are presented in this essay to support Siddall's claim that the Player King's speech is of central importance to *Hamlet*?

Kate Flint

*Kate Flint is Fellow in English
Literature at Mansfield College, Oxford,
and the author of numerous critical
studies.*

ESSAY

Madness and melancholy in *Hamlet*

'Turbulent and dangerous lunacy' (III.1.4); 'crafty madness' (III.1.8). Hamlet, in the eyes of those who observe his behaviour during the central Acts of the play, is far from being in his perfect mind.

These observers oscillate in their assessments, however — unable to agree whether his disturbed and antisocial behaviour is a genuine ailment or a put-up job, an entirely manufactured 'antic disposition'. Moreover, they debate whether his symptoms are those of madness itself, when the harmonious 'noble and most sovereign reason' (III.1.159) falls violently into disarray, or whether, on the other hand, Hamlet suffers from what might more accurately be termed 'melancholy'. This condition was, for Hamlet's contemporaries, much more amenable than madness to the analysis of reason itself. Also, because of its close connection with excitement or disappointment in love, 'melancholy' offers a framework of explanation which at first can be made to explain and contain Hamlet's behaviour in domestic terms: 'the very ecstasy of love,/ Whose violent property fordoes itself/ And leads the will to desperate undertakings' (II.1.102–104).

But Ophelia's description of reason in terms of kingly qualities (III.1.158) alerts us to the equation which is made throughout the play between sanity and fitness to rule. Hamlet's disorder not only transgresses acceptable aristocratic behaviour but can be spoken of as something threatening the well-being of the state as well as of the individual. Ophelia's own affliction provides a useful point of contrast with the Prince. When she has broken down, in IV.5, her songs and speech have an internal logic, revealed through her obsession with abandoned maids, false love, and memory. 'A document in madness: thoughts and remembrance fitted' (IV.5.179–180), comments Laertes on her pointed distribution of flowers and herbs. Yet, self-enclosed, her words lack those connections with other protagonists which would involve and endanger anyone but herself: 'poor Ophelia' excites compassion, not personal anxiety. On the other hand, Claudius observing Hamlet remarks, with concern for his own position, that 'what he spake, though it lacked form a little,/ Was not like madness. There's something in his soul/ O'er which his melancholy sits on brood' (III.1.164–166).

Deviance from a behavioural norm was frequently, in the Renaissance period, described in physical terms, as the over-preponderance of a 'humour' or 'complexion' — of blood, choler, melancholy or phlegm — in the body — state's defensive mechanism: the 'o'ergrowth of some complexion,/ Oft breaking down the pales and forts of reason' (I.4.27–28). Shakespeare's audience, like Claudius, would have had little trouble in identifying as the attributes of melancholy, the peculiarities which, in calculated or involuntary fashion, set Hamlet apart.

Timothy Bright's *Treatise of Melancholy* (1586), a possible if not provable influence on Shakespeare, provides ready evidence of how this fashionable malady could be recognised:

> The perturbations of melancholy are for the most part sad and fearful ... as distrust, doubt, diffidence, or despair, sometimes furious, and sometimes merry in appearance, through a kind of Sardonian [sardonic], and false laughter, as the humour is disposed that procureth these diversions.

Hamlet bids the court, and us, to be wary of his initial display of mourning. His trappings and suits of woe, his sighs and his 'dejected 'haviour of the visage' (I.2.81) are enumerated by him as stagy outward tokens of grief. His protestation that he has 'that within which passes show' (I.2.85), existing independently of these gloomy tokens, alerts us, even before he has grounds for dissembling, that surface manifestations need bear little relation to genuine feeling. But the symptoms which he goes on to display — his distrust and doubt at the Ghost's words or over Ophelia's purity, his despair at his own inability to act, his fury over his mother's remarriage and his sardonic jesting with the Players and with Rosencrantz and Guildenstern — add up to an almost text-book type of the melancholic. His very desire for drama, whether created by himself or by others, finds its place in Bright, where comedy is described as a standard cure both for melancholy and for the melancholic's inability to adjust to his situation, and where a rapid alternation of intense despondency with inappropriate frivolity and joke-cracking itself is put forward as another symptom:

> If bloud minister matter to this fire, every serious thing for a time, is turned into a jest, & tragedies into comedies, and lamenting into gigges and daunces. . . .

To discuss Hamlet's behaviour in these terms, of madness and sanity, or melancholy versus calm, balanced rationality, is, however, to fall into a trap: a trap of believing that such classifications can easily, or profitably be drawn. It is to stay, virtually, within Renaissance categories of explanation. These are essential if we are to understand how some of Shakespeare's original audience may have viewed the play, but inadequate as a complete description of the way its language functions.

Early psychoanalytic discussion of *Hamlet* centres around what Freud calls the Prince's 'neurotic symptoms', particularly as they affect the delay in killing Claudius. Capable of action in almost all circumstances, his repressed Oedipal complex prevents him, we are told in chapter 5 of *The Interpretation of Dreams*, from taking:

> . . . vengeance on the man who did away with his father and took that father's place with his mother, the man who shows him the repressed wishes of his own childhood realized. Thus the loathing which should drive him on to revenge is replaced in him by self-reproaches, by scruples of conscience, which remind

him that he himself is literally no better than the sinner whom he is to punish.

But such interpretation approaches Hamlet as though he, and the other characters, are 'real' people, not textual and dramatic constructs. We cannot place a character in a play or a novel on a couch and ask searching questions of them; they have no past, no parenthood except in the imaginations of their creator and those who subsequently read of them. Yet this does not mean that we should disallow the insights and terminology of psychoanalysis in our reading of literature. What I propose is a modern psychoanalytic reading of *Hamlet* which allows us to focus on the impossibility of ever defining who or what a 'real' person is, in or out of a text. It challenges the concept of there being a stable norm of personality, against which deviations, named 'madness' or 'melancholy', may be measured.

In order to survive and succeed in the unstable world of political intrigue which is presented in *Hamlet*, it is necessary, the play suggests, to be capable of maintaining both to oneself and others, the belief that one can achieve the status of a fully integrated human subject: one whose character can be referred to as a constant, which does not alter unduly with circumstance, which does not betray the pressures of the unconscious continually rising up within and against the conscious being. This ideal condition is one which Hamlet envies in the steady Horatio, whom he speaks of as a man 'Whose blood and judgement are so well commeddled/ That they are not a pipe for Fortune's finger/ To sound what stop she please' (III.2.79–81). Fortinbras — obeying codes of daring and honour, and not suffering as Hamlet does from qualms of 'conscience', or thinking too precisely about what to do, rather than getting on with the necessary action — ends as confident possessor of the state, confirming his authority through ordering an outward show of funereal ceremony which reveals nothing of the thoughts and feelings of the man within. Like, say, *Richard II*, the play dramatises the links between the body private, inevitably divided against itself, and the body politic, which must consciously suppress such division in order to preserve its stability.

As we saw earlier, to assume that one can tell when

someone is 'mad' and when he or she is 'sane' involves the formation and application of classifications and categories, whether these categories are couched in Renaissance or later terms. In *Hamlet*, this categorisation is most frequently performed through characters' confident separation of rational discrimination on the one hand and irrationality on the other, as when Claudius describes the distraught Ophelia:

> Divided from herself and her fair judgement,
> Without the which we are pictures or mere beasts.
>
> (IV.5.86–87)

Hamlet himself makes expeditious use of the conventions which equate sanity with identity, and which describe the disturbed body as a state divided against itself, when he apologises to Laertes:

> What I have done
> That might your nature, honour, and exception
> Roughly awake, I here proclaim was madness.
> Was't Hamlet wronged Laertes? Never Hamlet.
> If Hamlet from himself be ta'en away,
> And when he's not himself does wrong Laertes,
> Then Hamlet does it not. Hamlet denies it.
> Who does it then? His madness. If't be so,
> Hamlet is of the faction that is wronged.
> His madness is poor Hamlet's enemy.
>
> (V.2.224–233)

But, just because the logic, as well as the honourable status of this public declaration is clear, there is no compulsion on us to take it as the utterance of the 'true' man, at last returned to his 'godlike reason'. To elevate logic and clarity above other forms of expression is, after all, to deny the force of Hamlet's — and Shakespeare's — allusive, metaphoric language: that quality of language which, in fact, most conspicuously marks off the Prince's identity from that of the play's other protagonists.

This is brought home only twenty lines later, when Laertes is disconcerted by the open-endedness of extravagant terms which may be compliment, may be satire:

HAMLET I'll be your foil, Laertes. In mine ignorance

> Your skill shall, like a star i'th'darkest night,
>   Stick fiery off indeed.
>
> LAERTES   You mock me, sir.
>
> (V.2.249–251)

The inseparable mingling of rationality and emotion in Hamlet's language throughout the play; the ability Shakespeare gives him to find metaphors which describe the most repulsive forms of corruption or which convey extremes of confusion and self-doubt, makes it impossible to adhere to Claudius's categorical belief that the irrational, the expression of one who lacks 'fair judgement', automatically deprives one of a 'soul'.

What is more, Hamlet's behaviour, his 'madness', allows him to disrupt other categories besides those of sanity and derangement. It gives him the licence of a fool to speak cruel truths, transgressing the language of social decorum which would normally be expected from a royal prince. These truths may link the private and the political, as when Hamlet runs verbal rings round Rosencrantz, exposing his disloyal friend as a sponge which soaks up the King's favour and rewards. In a sequence which has social implications reaching far beyond the action on stage, Hamlet taunts Claudius's political ambition by claiming that 'a king may go a progress through the guts of a beggar' (IV.3.29–30). As he reminds one of the levelling effects of death, a familiar piece of sermonising for his audience, the thought behind his 'wild and whirling' words here is indistinguishable from his sombre, 'sane' discourse when, in Act V, he and the gravediggers discuss the fate of Yorick, the actual court fool of the past, whose function has been filled by Hamlet's serious jesting. Although the brain's earthly home is no more, in death, than a smelly skull, Hamlet uses his homily to drive home the poetic and political importance of stretching one's mental faculties in life: 'Why may not imagination trace the noble dust of Alexander till 'a find it stopping a bunghole?' (V.1.199–201).

Through his foolery, Hamlet does more than act as a moral and political commentator. He also breaks down a further distinction, that between player and audience. This relationship is foregrounded in the play in any case, of course, with the presence of the Players, and *The Murder of Gonzago*. Hamlet's 'antic disposition' not only highlights the difficulty of discerning what is and is not acting: it also puts him into the position, at times, of chorus, commenting on the action, a sardonic bridge between play-characters and audience. Moreover, his language, particularly in his 'madness', whilst rich and allusive, is by no means exclusively aristocratic. He uses more puns than any other Shakespearean figure. Over half the proverbial sayings in the play are uttered by him. Some of these ambiguously cover more than one social world. To know 'a hawk from a handsaw' (II.2.378) is to speak both the language of court falconry — to be able to tell a hawk from a heron — and of the ordinary workman: to distinguish between a plasterer's mortar board and a hand-saw. Hamlet's rapid, quibbling speech is seldom totally, or even partially understood by his companions on stage — a dramatic tactic to make one wonder whether to call someone mad is, at times, no more than to refuse to admit to one's own limitations.

Definitions and categories have their uses. Above all, to employ them is to be sure of one's self and of one's own capacity to judge, to use one's reason: to be confident, therefore, of one's own sanity. Whether the Prince of Denmark is in his perfect mind, or whether he is suffering from extremes of emotion so intense that other characters find it easiest, for private or political motives, to deal with them by safely consigning them to the area of madness or intense melancholy matters little: to worry about this is to believe in the dramatic persona as a 'real' character who can be analysed, described, contained. Those stage characters who think of Hamlet as mad illustrate this perfectly: they are mostly motivated by self-interest, or suffer from wishing their own particular image of the Prince to be confirmed, or from a lack of intellectual sharpness. Yet we should not presume ourselves to be in some peculiarly privileged position when it comes to identifying the 'real' Hamlet. The figure remains unpredictable, sometimes opaque. What his so-called madness does, however, do, is to make one realise the danger of equating stable, self-consistent and unimaginative characters with the possession of sanity: to presume that we can determine what is 'normal', and therefore 'real', with regard to any figure, fictional or otherwise. This caution which Shakespeare's play induces, this admission that a fully controlled, self-knowing, self-integrated human subject is ultimately a chimera holds true whether we consider the judgements of the characters in the play, the Renaissance audience, or ourselves.

AFTERTHOUGHTS

1

Explain the Renaissance concept of 'melancholy' as outlined on pages 62–63. What, according to Flint, are the limitations of discussing Hamlet's character with reference to such terms?

2

What arguments does Flint give against accepting 'early psychoanalytic discussion' of *Hamlet* (page 63)? Compare her comments here with the points made by Selden on pages 81–90.

3

Why does Flint argue that Hamlet's use of puns is significant (page 67)?

4

What distinctions are drawn in this essay between madness and sanity?

William Tydeman
*William Tydeman lectures in English at
the University College of Wales at
Bangor.*

ESSAY

The case of
the wicked uncle

The other morning, instead of sitting down and reading *Hamlet*,
I sat down and read a detective story. Most readers will recognise the mood I was in, the one in which the great peaks of world
literature no longer produce inspiration but altitude-sickness,
and we descend to the literary chip-shop in the valley for a brief
rest. I didn't choose a particularly good detective story, and yet
I just had to read through to the last chapter to find out (along
with Inspector Blunder of the Yard) who precisely among the
Fearnley-Whittingstalls' repulsive house-guests had skewered
the blonde model to the diving board in the swimming pool with
a halberd stolen from the Tower of London. And when I eventually got back to *Hamlet*, I couldn't entirely forget the detective
story — not so much the sinister Hungarian butler or the
missing Cabinet Minister or even the blonde, but Inspector
Blunder, CID, who in the best Scotland Yard tradition didn't
succeed in tracking down the killer and revealing his identity
until the book's final chapter when he gathered all the surviving
characters together in the library and explained his deductions.

And I fell to wondering why it was that I'd always accepted
without question that until the very end Blunder would make
mistakes and draw wrong conclusions, follow false trails and

come up against blank walls, suspect the guest with the perfect alibi, have the most vital piece of evidence stolen from his bedroom, and so on. Why was it that I hadn't once demanded that Inspector Blunder should solve the crime more vigorously, more cleverly, or more swiftly? Surely the answer was that I'd tacitly recognised the conventions of the genre, which dictated that Blunder should not resolve the mystery until the moment of truth in chapter 36, because, if the light had dawned in that slow, methodical mind any sooner, my pleasure would have come to an abrupt end? There had been a silent agreement between the author and myself that my willingness to keep reading depended on an awareness of the fact that Blunder would only get it right when we arrived at page 242 and not before. It was part of a pre-established routine which I'd taken on trust as innocently as a small child might.

And wasn't it also significant that I'd never once attempted in the course of my reading to attribute Inspector Blunder's failure to identify the criminal until the ultimate chapter to some hidden psychological motive or weakness in his personal character? I had again taken it as axiomatic that Blunder's tardy revelation of the truth had nothing to do with inadequacy or irresolution or a near-fatal fondness for Bourbon biscuits; his creator had deliberately strewn obstacles and hazards in Blunder's way, not to make points about his personality or temperament, but in order to prevent the discovery of the murderer's identity until the last possible moment. Blunder's idiosyncratic quirks of behaviour — his fear of heights, his habit of chewing a daisy as he paced the lawn planning the next move, his dislike of eating in Little Chefs — were no doubt part of his appeal, but they had no real bearing on his inability to complete his case until the appropriate time. His traits of character had nothing to do with his conventional function.

In the past it has often been customary for readers and critics to assume that *Hamlet* is predominantly a study of the character of its protagonist, and that its principal interest lies in the attempt to elucidate exactly why Hamlet finds himself unable to carry out the instruction of his father's ghost to:

Revenge his foul and most unnatural murder.

(I.5.25)

Much speculation and research have been devoted to establishing what constitutes the precise 'flaw' in the Prince's nature which the task of vengeance enjoined upon him exposes, and Hamlet's famous lines on those noble personalities vitiated by a single fault have been taken to reflect Shakespeare's recognition of his hero's own Achilles heel:

> So oft it chances in particular men
> That for some vicious mole of nature in them,
> As in their birth, wherein they are not guilty,
> Since nature cannot choose his origin —
> By the o'ergrowth of some complexion,
> Oft breaking down the pales and forts of reason,
> Or by some habit, that too much o'erleavens
> The form of plausive manners — that these men,
> Carrying, I say, the stamp of one defect,
> Being nature's livery or fortune's star,
> His virtues else, be they as pure as grace,
> As infinite as man may undergo,
> Shall in the general censure take corruption
> From that particular fault.

(I.4.23–36)

I want to challenge the still far from defunct notion that Shakespeare's sole preoccupation is with Hamlet's complex individual psychology and that the play's success relies on its author's capacity to create a coherent account of how Hamlet's 'fatal flaw' affects his fate. I do not believe that Hamlet's personality can ever be 'explained' in a totally satisfactory manner — Shakespeare was not a late-nineteenth-century novelist — but more importantly, I would argue that we do violence to this majestic masterpiece if we approach it obsessed with the idea that it seeks to present a diagnosis of a 'mixed-up' personality. Sir Walter Scott in the preface to *The Talisman* (1825) wrote of a playbill 'said to have announced the tragedy of Hamlet, the character of the Prince of Denmark being left out', and we might do well to consider Shakespeare's play for once, not without 'the character of the Prince of Denmark', which would be manifestly absurd, but without regarding this element as the only focus of interest in the drama which bears his name.

I am far from suggesting that *Hamlet* is nothing more than an Elizabethan detective story and therefore subject to identical conventions to those which I sketched in at the opening of this essay. But I do suggest that an approach to *Hamlet* which acknowledges that even the greatest masterpieces of world literature are subject to certain laws and assumptions, may cast a more helpful light on such works than that shed by means of the implicit belief that major writers are exempt from such restraints. Among the innumerable explanations advanced to account for Hamlet's so-called 'delay' in dispatching his uncle — melancholia, religious scruples, moral cowardice, scholarly wimpishness, Freudian neurosis, habits of procrastination, doubts as to the Ghost's integrity — it is easy to lose sight of the one obvious certainty: Hamlet cannot sweep to his revenge for much the same reasons that Inspector Blunder cannot solve the murder mystery by the end of chapter 4. The conventions will not permit him to do so: the dramatic action must be sustained for the required period of time, or the demands of the form (and those of the public) will remain unsatisfied. As Sir Thomas Hanmer wrote in his *Remarks on the Tragedy of Hamlet* in 1736:

> Had Hamlet gone naturally to work, as we could suppose such a Prince to do in parallel Circumstances, there would have been an End of our Play.

Perhaps Hanmer's common-sense view depends too much on the assumption that Hamlet is fashioned in the mould of a stereotyped princess-rescuing prince of tradition, but his recognition of the impossibility of a swift decisive response to the Ghost's injunction does him credit amid the welter of alternative explanations advanced since his day.

However, it is fair to admit that Hanmer, having recognised that 'The Poet . . . was obliged to delay his Hero's Revenge', goes on to maintain that Shakespeare had failed to provide 'some good Reason' for the hold-up. As far as an Elizabethan audience was concerned, it is doubtful whether its members would have been perturbed by what Hanmer and many of his successors interpreted later as a lack of motivation. The story of Hamlet, as it had been transmitted to the playwrights of sixteenth-century England from the Danish historian Saxo Grammaticus via the French writer François de Belleforest, in around 1570, was one in which suspense, stratagem, and temporising were taken for granted, the primary interest residing in waiting to see if Amleth Prince of Jutland would succeed in convincing his father's murderer Fengo that he was truly mad and therefore harmless, then whether he would manage to evade his evil uncle's traps and so eventually survive to accomplish his mission of vengeance before Fengo could have him eliminated. At the conclusion Saxo comments on the factors leading to the hero's success:

> ... one and all rested the greatest hope on his wisdom, since he had devised the whole of such an achievement with the deepest cunning, and accomplished it with the most astonishing contrivance. Many could have been seen marvelling how he had concealed so subtle a plan over so long a space of time.

'Cunning', 'contrivance', concealment and subtlety exercised over a long 'space of time' were thus the keynotes of the Hamlet narrative in its earliest forms, and it is worth noting how Shakespeare treats the ingredients which contributed to that impression. He certainly increases the tension by beginning the play with Hamlet as ignorant of the true circumstances of his father's death, as are the Danish people:

> So the whole ear of Denmark
> Is by a forgèd process of my death
> Rankly abused

(I.5.36–38)

and by introducing a ghost (a device possibly invented by the anonymous author of a lost *Hamlet*) to inform the Prince of Claudius's secret act of treachery by poison. By this means an audience can share the shock of Hamlet's discovery of the true state of affairs, while the clandestine nature of Claudius's crime by contrast with Fengo's public act at a banquet initiates the programme of stealth and deception. Amleth's feigned madness is preserved in Hamlet's 'antic disposition', and the cat-and-mouse tactics between king and nephew mirror Fengo's efforts to ascertain the true condition of Amleth's mind. The unscrupulous use of Ophelia as decoy by the King and her father parallels similar incidents in Saxo and Belleforest; the killing of Polonius is analogous, as are the journey to England with the two treacherous friends and the return to exact justice, even if the savage reprisals taken by the primitive Prince of Jutland — massacre and arson — are moderated in Hamlet's more refined retribution package. Nearly all the staple elements of the known plot are retained in deference to the spectators' expectations that *Hamlet* will necessarily involve a display of guile, ingenuity and caution. To them the narrative pattern dictated that prolongation of the suspense was a prerequisite of any dramatic action based upon it, and provided in itself sufficient 'good Reason' for the 'delay'.

It is legitimate to argue, however, that whatever his first audiences may have expected of the Hamlet story, Shakespeare provided them with a bonus in the shape of a tragic protagonist far more complex and 'characterful' than his prototypes, perhaps far more 'characterful' and complex than the plot material truly required. It is not unusual for critics to draw attention to alleged discrepancies between the crude devices of situation and plot that the playwright inherited and the subtleties of characterisation and expression which he deployed to animate and illuminate them. T S Eliot even went so far as to pronounce *Hamlet* an 'artistic failure' on the grounds that its situations (for example the death of a beloved father) did not justify the emotional responses they called forth. Given that Shakespeare appears to give Hamlet psychological burdens to bear as well as physical obstacles to overcome, we may reasonably seek to discover how far those personal qualities actually influence the necessary process of lingering out the assassination of Claudius until Act V, scene 2.

As we saw, previous Hamlets had been expected to scheme and act cunningly on the path successfully to avenge a parent's murder, Saxo's Amleth simulating madness lest Fengo should suspect him of planning revenge. Shakespeare, however, appears to have other reasons for having Hamlet adopt his 'antic disposition', since attendant circumstances certainly do not justify it: Claudius's villainy is not public knowledge like Fengo's, and hence he has no reason to suspect his nephew as had the original usurper. Ironically, Shakespeare makes Hamlet's 'transformation' attract the royal suspicion rather than allay it, since from it stem the summoning of Rosencrantz and Guildenstern and the decision to ship the Prince to England. We often forget that Claudius resolves on this move before the play-scene and the murder of Polonius strengthen his purpose, being convinced that:

> There's something in his soul
> O'er which his melancholy sits on brood,
> And I do doubt the hatch and the disclose
> Will be some danger . . .
>
> Haply the seas, and countries different,
> With variable objects, shall expel
> This something-settled matter in his heart,
> Whereon his brains still beating puts him thus
> From fashion of himself . . .

(III.1.165–168, 172–176)

Whether at this point Claudius is taken in or not is unclear; he argues in lines 164–166 that Hamlet does not seem mad despite his wild words, yet his parting remark is to say that 'Madness in great ones must not unwatched go', though this may be a ruse to hide his deeper anxieties from Polonius.

At all events, at this critical juncture the personal characteristics bestowed on Hamlet can hardly be held to be a potent force in assisting the 'delaying tactics' called for: it is the traditional assumption of madness, not mental or emotional factors, which keeps Hamlet from his prey by alerting the King. Moreover, the feigned insanity seems at odds with the hero's astuteness manifested elsewhere. Had Shakespeare not had him adopt the guise of madman, Hamlet's opportunities for displaying that blend of caution and contrivance so admired in Amleth might have been developed, and the King's suspicions never aroused until he felt Hamlet's rapier in his heart. To this extent, then, the 'primitive' inheritance served to undermine much of the mental and emotional sophistication with which the Elizabethan fleshed out his protagonist.

Some episodes in Shakespeare's play were doubtless included in its lost predecessor, and one novelty was the introduction to Elsinore of the Players and the court performance of *The Mousetrap* before the guilty King. Critics maintain that this innovation is a clear indication of the importance for the action of Hamlet's character, since to them the presence of the dramatic presentation offers further proof that this is a study of a classic procrastinator or of an unstable personality. But we do not necessarily need to assume some deep psychological motive for what the Prince makes the Players do: not only is it a device for advancing the action, but again Hamlet's plan to 'catch the conscience of the King' works against psychological plausibility, since its curious ineptitude reveals to Claudius Hamlet's knowledge of the crime he has committed. The play-scene is an ingenious invention and makes for excellent theatre, but one may doubt whether it should be viewed as resulting from a subtle piece of characterisation.

Another Elizabethan importation is the scene in which Hamlet finds the King at prayer, but forbears to kill him then and there. Here Shakespeare is under no pressure from inherited precedents, but is able to ground the arguments Hamlet advances for sparing Claudius in such character traits as he gives the Prince. Many have been the accusations of inadequacy and evasiveness heaped on Hamlet for his conduct at this crisis in the action, and his reasoning is frequently seen as an attempt to rationalise a craven disinclination to kill a fellow-creature. But this interpretation fails to square with the sentiments expressed: admittedly, unlike the more impetuous Laertes on a later occasion, Hamlet does 'scan', or scrutinise carefully, what he proposes to do, namely slay a praying man and so ensure his passage to heaven, in the full knowledge that his own murdered father is enduring the agonies of 'sulphurous and tormenting flames' in purgatory. He rejects the idea that adequate compensation would be exacted if he dispatched Claudius:

> . . . in the purging of his soul,
> When he is fit and seasoned for his passage

(III.3.85–86)

But his reason for sparing him is not an act of timidity or procrastination, but rather a calculated resolve to make his uncle suffer as his father is suffering, by performing his duty at some less hallowed moment:

> When he is drunk asleep, or in his rage,
> Or in th'incestuous pleasure of his bed,
> At game, a-swearing, or about some act

That has no relish of salvation in't —
Then trip him, that his heels may kick at heaven
And that his soul may be as damned and black
As hell, whereto it goes.

(III.3.89–95)

Yet even here it may be claimed that the characterisation has been called forth by the situation rather than the other way around: the image of the determined, remorseless avenger biding his time is certainly at odds with the weak vacillator depicted in Hamlet's self-portraits which receive so much critical attention. It seems clear that it suited Shakespeare's purposes at this point in the action to stress a fresh aspect of Hamlet's many-sided personality for no other reason than to retard the action once again.

It is hard to resist the view that for much of the time what happens to Hamlet happens not because Hamlet is given the kind of personality he has — and we shall argue for ever as to what kind of personality that is — but because the main feature of the storyline — the postponement of the processes of revenge — is laid down already. Hamlet's 'character' often appears to exist independent of the events which occur — the feigned madness, the rejection of Ophelia, the stabbing of Polonius, the voyage to England, the removal of the former companions, the capture by pirates, the return to Denmark, the fatal duel with Laertes. None of these incidents occurs as a direct outcome of any positive or negative qualities of personality which we may be invited to attribute to Hamlet. What we learn of the multi-faceted qualities of the hero's psychological make-up seems to me to stand independent of the salient events unfolded.

What then of the anguish of the Prince, what of those celebrated soliloquies in which he unpacks his heart with words and so reveals to us his most intimate feelings, his self-doubts, his loss of mirth, his self-disgust, his sense of world-weary inadequacy? Are they irrelevant to the play? Are these intense expressions of insight into an angry, lonely, disappointed, despairing mind excrescences on the surface of a mere adventure-story? The answer is self-evidently in the negative. These things are among the chief rewards in reading *Hamlet* or seeing it on stage. But it is almost as if we were dealing with two different plays: one the interior drama of Hamlet's mind, in which he broods on his inability to cope with his allotted task; the other a drama of externals, in which a tragic hero is frustrated by physical circumstances, including the accident of encountering Claudius at prayer rather than at play. While we receive from Hamlet's soliloquies the data which enable us to accuse him (if we choose) of irresolution, cowardice, infirmity of purpose, instability, excessive passion, of all those human frailties which have helped to substantiate the time-honoured charge that he 'delays', the action itself fails to register this impression on us. It is only Hamlet himself who believes that he is 'A dull and muddy-mettled rascal' (though the Ghost does refer in Act III, scene 4 to his 'almost blunted purpose'); it does not find a place in Horatio's catalogue:

> Of carnal, bloody, and unnatural acts,
> Of accidental judgements, casual slaughters,
> Of deaths put on by cunning and forced cause,
> And, in this upshot, purposes mistook
> Fallen on th'inventors' heads.

(V.2.375–379)

It seems permissible to argue that Hamlet, set before us as a vibrant and vivid creation, is none the less a dramatic figure whose personal psychology plays a far less central part in the unfolding of his story than is often assumed. Penetrating as are the insights into the human condition which his long speeches offer us, to identify the theme of the play as residing in an exploration of the nexus achieved between his personality and the action in which he participates is misleading. In the final critical analysis Hamlet is called upon to fulfil a functional role every bit as prescribed as that of our old friend Inspector Blunder of the Yard.

AFTERTHOUGHTS

1

How would you describe the tone and content of the first three paragraphs of this essay? Do you find this approach helpful?

2

How useful do you find it to be made aware of the source material for *Hamlet* (pages 73–76)?

3

Do you agree with T S Eliot's comments about *Hamlet* (page 75)?

4

What answers would you give to the questions posed by Tydeman at the beginning of the penultimate paragraph of this essay?

Raman Selden

Raman Selden is Professor of English Literature at the University of Lancaster, and the author of numerous critical studies.

ESSAY

Hamlet's word-play and the Oedipus complex

Sophocles' play *Oedipus Tyrannus* concentrates only on the central crisis in the myth. The whole story can be told briefly. Laius, King of Thebes, is told by an oracle that his son will kill his father and marry his mother Jocasta. Laius abandons the child, Oedipus, on Mount Cithaeron, but a shepherd rescues him and hands him over to Polybus, King of Corinth, who brings the child up as his own. Hearing of the oracle, Oedipus flees, assuming Polybus is his father. On the way to Thebes he unwittingly kills Laius at a cross-road. Arriving at Thebes he saves the city by solving the riddle of the Sphinx. Later, having unknowingly married his mother, who bears him children, Oedipus consults the oracle about a plague afflicting the city. He is told of the blood-guiltiness which must be purged. He vows to hunt down the criminal, little knowing that it is he himself. When finally bit by bit the truth dawns upon him, Jocasta commits suicide and Oedipus blinds himself.

Sigmund Freud believed that the myth of Oedipus possessed a profound insight into an important stage in the psychological development of human beings. He suggested that all sons go through a phase in their childhood when they desire to kill their fathers and marry their mothers. There is a complementary but more complex route followed by girls (and since Hamlet is male, we will stick to the male route). This desire is *unconscious* but none the less real in its effects. It marks an early stage in the child's development towards adult sexuality. Hitherto, the child, in the pre-Oedipal phase, has been oriented solely towards his mother. In the new phase, the father becomes 'rival' for his mother's affections. The threat of 'castration' (loss of male organs) forces the son to abandon his incestuous desire for his mother (all in the unconscious). The son now identifies with the father and perceives him as a role model rather than as a rival. In this way the transition to adult life and a mature male identity is achieved. However, as many of Freud's case studies show, the Oedipal phase is not completely surpassed, because the abandonment of mother love is achieved only by *repression* of unconscious desire. Repressed desires never go away: they remain latent, waiting for moments of crisis in the life of the adult. In other words, there is a price to pay for successful maturation. If the Oedipus complex is not successfully overcome the son will preserve an unhealthy love for the mother and will find transition to heterosexual love difficult.

The relevance of Freud's theory of the Oedipus complex to *Hamlet* is fairly obvious, and Freud himself was the first to point it out in 'Psychopathic Characters on the Stage' (*c.* 1905). He argues that, like all mature males, Hamlet must have passed through the Oedipal phase and effectively repressed his Oedipal desires, but a crisis occurs in his life which brings the repressed desires to the surface again, totally disrupting Hamlet's ability to act. Hamlet is not aware of this damaging conflict inside himself, but he reveals its existence to the audience through certain symptoms in his behaviour and language. In his famous *Hamlet and Oedipus* (London, 1949), Ernest Jones developed Freud's brief treatment of the play.

Jones speculates that Hamlet had repressed his Oedipal feelings in adulthood so successfully that his admiration and love of his father were the most prominent features of his filial emotions. Near the beginning of the play, Hamlet hears from the Ghost the news that his father was murdered. This realisation of his earliest childhood wish (to kill his father), which had been repressed so thoroughly, suddenly revives in him Oedipal thoughts of incest and parricide. In his reading of the play, Jones explains Hamlet's delay in psychological terms. Hamlet identifies himself with Claudius, because he did the thing which the son unconsciously desired to do. His guilty feelings (expressed by the Ghost) move him to plan revenge on Claudius, but he desists, because in killing Claudius he would be killing himself, since he too unconsciously wished to kill the King.

Avi Erlich, in *Hamlet's Absent Father* (1977), argues that it would make more sense for Hamlet to mitigate his guilt by killing Claudius, because, in any case, Hamlet's true identification is not with Claudius but with his father. Erlich explains the psychological problem as follows: 'Every boy may wish to kill his father, but, more importantly, every boy needs a strong father to make him give up his incest fantasies and go on to be a strong man like his father.' The real conflict in Hamlet, according to Erlich, is between his idealised image of the father and the actual impotence and badness of his father. When he decides not to kill Claudius at his prayers, Hamlet refers to his father's being killed when he was 'full of bread' (sensual appetites) and 'With all his crimes broad blown' (III.3.80–81). Hamlet prefers to await a more pious moment to murder Claudius; he really wants to have Claudius punished by a just God (another strong father figure), who could not be expected to support revenge upon a man at prayer (ironically, Claudius is in fact in a state of total spiritual despair). Laertes does not have these conflicts about Polonius, his dead father, and can act and discourse about his revenge without inner conflict.

There are, of course, many other explanations of Hamlet's delay, several of which make some sense. For example, it can be argued that he has profound moral scruples about revenge and that his feelings about this are not unlike the official Christian condemnation of revenge as an immoral act. Alternatively, it has been argued that Hamlet has by nature a reflective disposition: he is inclined to thought rather than action. A third possibility is that he is melancholy by nature, suffers distracting thoughts of suicide and black ideas of human wickedness, all of which disable him and prevent action. These are only some of the suggestions which have been made by critics. What reasons can one find in the play to justify supporting the psychological types of explanation we have been discussing? Are we justified in adopting an evidently *modern* type of explanation when discussing a Renaissance play?

The central feature of Hamlet's behaviour which requires explanation is his so-called 'madness'. The problem is that, even though he announces his intention (to Horatio) to assume 'an antic disposition', there are scenes in the play in which Hamlet appears to be genuinely deranged (especially in his interviews with Ophelia and during the gravediggers' scene when he confronts Laertes). It may be impossible to determine whether Hamlet's derangement is genuine or not in some parts of the play. However, the question still arises, what sort of madness is it (whether assumed or real)?

If we adopt a 'historical' view, we would expect Hamlet's 'madness' to be fully explicable in terms of Renaissance psychology and medicine. This approach insists that only those theories available to Shakespeare's contemporaries are relevant to an understanding of Shakespeare's texts. Hamlet's melancholy has been seized on as an explanation of his inclination to madness. The 'malady' of melancholy was much discussed in the Elizabethan period. Hamlet himself talks of the theory of 'humours' according to which an individual's character may be dominated by an imbalance in his 'complexion' (disposition). The melancholy man has an excess of black bile in his 'complexion', which creates a certain behaviour pattern. Timothy Bright's *Treatise of Melancholy* (1586) tells us that the melancholy man is given to 'contemplation' and is 'not so apt for action': 'The perturbations of melancholy are for the most part sad and fearful, and such as rise of them: as distrust, doubt, diffidence, or despair, sometimes furious, and sometimes merry in appearance, through a kind of Sardonian [sardonic], and false laughter'. Hamlet's behaviour clearly follows this pattern. As Harold Jenkins says (in the Arden edition of the play), there is no reason to suppose that Shakespeare had read Bright, since these ideas were commonplace. Indeed any account of Hamlet's 'madness' which reduces his remarkable and unique patterns of discourse to a commonplace malady will lack conviction. One might add that it is not safe to treat Hamlet's presented behaviour as in some sense his native disposition. After all, he has immediate *reasons* to be melancholy and also explicitly tells us that he is going intentionally to behave oddly. It would be more reasonable to say that Hamlet *assumes* characteristics of the melancholy type as the foundation of his 'antic disposition'. We may still have to leave open the possibility that he actually becomes deranged at certain points in the play.

There is a further aspect of his words to Horatio (I.5) that deserves emphasis. He announces that he will talk in 'doubtful' phraseology and will be 'ambiguous'. This side of his 'madness' has little to do with 'melancholy'. As will be made clear later, the most recent kinds of psychoanalytic criticism treat the slippery and playful features of language as a guide to the slippery and unstable nature of personality. Shakespeare produced many other characters who are fond of ambiguity and 'equivocation' (playing around with the meanings of words). The Elizabethan writers were generally addicted to word-play of all kinds. Modern readers are often less responsive to the pun and regard it as a low form of humour. Not so the Elizabethans, who relished a good pun. The word-play of Shakespeare's clowns often takes the form of their misdirection of others' words to their own purposes. There is something subversive in this slippery use of language: it is often used to reveal truths which ordinary language refuses to recognise. Of all Shakespeare's characters Hamlet is the master 'equivocator'. He recognises the power of equivocation when he complains of the gravedigger's use of it against him: 'We must speak by the card [unambiguously], or equivocation will undo us' (V.1.135–136). His own equivocations disturb, puzzle or irritate Gertrude, Claudius, Ophelia, Rosencrantz and Guildenstern. However, from a psychoanalytic viewpoint, we must add that Hamlet's word-play not only undermines the position of other people but, more importantly, it reveals Hamlet's own unconscious thoughts.

Polonius notes Hamlet's word-play and comments on the link between madness and cleverness with words: 'How pregnant sometimes his replies are! A happiness that often madness hits on' (II.2.208–210). However, Ophelia's madness, which drives her to harp on lost virginity and desertion, does not involve this cunning word-play. The Gentleman who reports to Gertrude Ophelia's distraction places a significant emphasis on her broken discourse — she:

> Spurns enviously at straws, speaks things in doubt

That carry but half sense. Her speech is nothing,
Yet the unshapèd use of it doth move
The hearers to collection. They aim at it,
And botch the words up fit to their own thoughts,
Which, as her winks and nods and gestures yield them,
Indeed would make one think there might be thought,
Though nothing sure . . .

(IV.5.6–13)

The model of verbal communication described here is antithetical to Hamlet's. Whereas he receives messages which he interprets and sends back transformed by equivocation, Ophelia's 'speech is nothing'. Her words lack coherence and require the listeners to piece them together to form meaningful utterances. Ophelia's speech demands that her listeners actively interpret it, while Hamlet's is a powerful interpretation of others' discourse. Her speech is full of gaps which require filling; Hamlet's speech is full of meaning, and resembles what Roland Barthes called a 'writerly' text, which encourages multiple interpretation. This fullness of meaning is what makes it possible to decipher messages from Hamlet's unconscious mind.

The following exchange between Hamlet and Claudius shows how disruptive Hamlet's word-play can be:

KING   How fares our cousin Hamlet?
HAMLET   Excellent, i'faith; of the chameleon's dish. I eat the air,
     promise-crammed. You cannot feed capons so.
KING   I have nothing with this answer, Hamlet. These words are
     not mine.
HAMLET   No, nor mine now.

(III.2.102–107)

Hamlet suggests that the words one utters immediately cease to be one's own property. They can be wrenched from their original context or intention and used for other purposes. This means that even though Hamlet's word-play gives him power over others, it is, in the end, not under his own control. A Freudian would say that when we make jokes or puns, and talk ambiguously, we are allowing unconscious thoughts to be expressed; we are permitting a temporary lifting of the censorship imposed by convention and by normal civilised restraints.

It has often been noticed that Hamlet seems to be obsessed

by sex. His mother's incestuous marriage to Claudius enflames his disgust. Does Hamlet's word-play relate to this Oedipal conflict? Two early examples of equivocation centre on the question of *kinship*:

> KING   But now, my cousin Hamlet, and my son —
> HAMLET (*aside*)   A little more than kin, and less than kind!
>
> (I.2.64–65)

Gertrude complains that he still seeks his 'noble father in the dust':

> QUEEN   Hamlet, thou hast thy father much offended.
> HAMLET   Mother, you have my father much offended.
> QUEEN   Come, come, you answer with an idle tongue.
>
> (III.4.10–12)

Hamlet declares he cannot forget that she is 'your husband's brother's wife' (III.4.16). The harping on this disturbance in proper relations of kinship centres on *incest*. The sexual intercourse between a wife and her husband's brother was regarded as incest in this period (Claudius refers openly to Gertrude as 'our sometime sister, now our queen'). Claudius is more than a mere kinsman ('cousin'); he has come uncomfortably close to Hamlet by marrying his mother, and yet is 'less than kind' (not his true father, with whom there would be the deep connections of family feeling). Hamlet's 'idle' (equivocal) tongue subversively identifies Old Hamlet and Claudius ('thy father' — 'my father'), thus drawing attention to a difference, but also revealing the uncertainty of Hamlet's position as a gendered 'subject' (the term 'subject' is used in modern critical theory to mean the 'first person' — 'I'). Hamlet's whole identity as a male 'subject' depended on his successful repression of his childish Oedipal desires. This repression is now in the process of being lifted, with devastating results.

Hamlet's disgust at Gertrude's 'incestuous' marriage is, from a Freudian viewpoint, a clear sign of his own Oedipal desire for his mother. His passionate and even violent behaviour towards her in the closet scene has all the marks of sexual jealousy. As Jacqueline Rose puts it, 'the violence towards the mother is the effect of the desire for her'. His dead father is no longer a rival, and now his own incestuous feelings are expressed through a bitter resentment of Claudius's actual 'incest'. He is horrified at the thought that his mother can feel sexual desire for Claudius:

> Nay, but to live
> In the rank sweat of an enseamèd bed,
> Stewed in corruption, honeying and making love
> Over the nasty sty —

(III.4.92–95)

Hamlet appears to have a lurid sense of his mother's actual physical lust, judging from his choice of words: 'sweat', 'enseamèd' (the word derives from 'seam' — animal fat), 'stewed' (with a play on 'stew', a brothel), and 'nasty sty'. He begs her to abstain from intercourse with Claudius. Hamlet's Oedipal feelings are revived by his mother's improperly directed sexuality. His excessive reaction is a symptom of this rekindling of the childhood instincts which should have remained repressed in the mature Hamlet.

Hamlet's preoccupation with incest is related to his general obsessive concern with sexuality. Disgust at Getrude's incestuous marriage drives him to see all sexuality as diseased and gross, and especially Ophelia's. Again his disgust is expressed in word-play: 'shall I lie in your lap? . . . Do you think I meant country [cunt-ry] matters?'

HAMLET   That's a fair thought — to lie between maids' legs.
OPHELIA   What is, my lord?
HAMLET   Nothing.

(III.2.121–130)

Hamlet's strange word-play includes a dimension which is illuminated by psychoanalysis. As editors have pointed out, 'nothing' can mean 'lack of the male "thing"', or the 'O' which lies between maids' legs. A possibly related passage is the one in which Hamlet confuses Rosencrantz and Guildenstern with word-play. When asked where the body is (Polonius's), Hamlet replies: 'The body is with the King, but the King is not with the body. The King is a thing — '. Guildenstern asks 'A thing, my lord?' Hamlet replies 'Of nothing'. (IV.2.27–30). Claudius has the male 'thing', which Hamlet would like to castrate and make a 'nothing'. Hamlet complains (III.4.101,103) to Gertrude that the King has pocketed 'the precious diadem' (taken the thing) and that he is 'A king of shreds and patches' (an image of castration) in contrast to the perfect image of the man that was his father.

Modern psychoanalytic criticism does not accept the way in which Freud and Jones treated characters as if they were real people. The only thing which psychoanalysis can examine, according to the French psychoanalyst Jacques Lacan, is 'textuality' itself — the discourse in which unconscious processes may be concealed. Lacan has argued, in his obscure but stimulating essay 'Desire and the Interpretation of Desire in *Hamlet*', that Hamlet's word-play is profoundly significant when trying to understand the psychological dimension of the play:

> One of Hamlet's functions is to engage in constant punning, word play, double-entendre — to play on ambiguity. Note that Shakespeare gives an essential role in his plays to those characters that are called fools, court jesters whose position allows them to uncover the most hidden motives, the character traits that cannot be discussed frankly without violating the norms of proper conduct. It's not a matter of mere impudence and insults. What they say proceeds basically by way of ambiguity, of metaphor, puns, conceits, mannered speech — those substitutions of signifiers whose essential function I have been stressing. Those substitutions lend Shakespeare's theatre a style, a color, that is the basis of its psychological dimension. Well, Hamlet, in a certain sense must be considered one of these clowns.
> *Literature and Psychoanalysis: The Question of Reading, Otherwise* ed Shoshana Felman — Baltimore 1982.

The unconscious mind makes itself manifest only in distorted forms (dreams, jokes, puns, slips of the tongue). Hamlet's repressed desires too come to the surface in this way. He himself states that he is aware of something going on in him which is more profound than his surface grief: 'But I have that within which passes show' (I.2.85). The externals of grief (black clothes, lamentation, tears) fail to 'denote' him (I.2.83). The only things which truly denote him are 'signifiers' (the actual words he utters, divorced from any fixed meanings). Hamlet knows that his mother's early remarriage to her dead husband's brother is deeply disturbing and offensive, but 'that within' shakes him so deeply that even in soliloquies he cannot bring if fully to consciousness.

Hamlet's 'antic disposition' is not just a device assumed for protection, but a psychological necessity. Unless the constraints of reason and custom are removed or loosened, unconscious desire cannot make itself known. After Polonius's death Claudius says of Hamlet, 'His liberty is full of threats to all' (IV.1.14). Hamlet is dangerous not just in the sense that he is plotting revenge, but because he has lifted the censorship which reason imposes on his repressed impulses. He feels he is a victim of passion and admires Horatio's stoicism: 'Give me the man/ That is not passion's slave'. Claudius is irritated by the irrational excess of Hamlet's grief which creates a dangerous and threatening atmosphere. Rosencrantz and Guildenstern are especially affected by Hamlet's 'liberty':

> GUILDENSTERN Good my lord, put your discourse into some frame, and start not so wildly from my affair. . . .
>
> HAMLET Sir, I cannot. . . . Make you a wholesome answer. My wit's diseased.
>
> (III.2.316–330)

His mind refuses to allow normal, conventional and restrained associations and reasonings to proceed. The flow of discourse is continually interrupted by the irrelevant but deeply significant deflections of the unconscious. If there is an Oedipal fixation in Hamlet, its symptoms are manifested in the slippery surface of his discourse where one may catch its reflection.

I have chosen to follow the Lacanian version of Freud's theory because it enables us to avoid speculating about Hamlet's family background or treating him as if he were a real person. We cannot ask Hamlet to lie on the psychoanalyst's couch and tell us his problems. However, we can detect the symptoms of his psychological problems in the very words he utters in the play. Hamlet's word-play is the key to his unconscious. What is revealed by a study of his equivocations is the lurking trauma of the Oedipus complex.

AFTERTHOUGHTS

1

To what extent has this essay clarified for you the concept of 'the Oedipus complex'?

2

Are the various explanations for Hamlet's behaviour given on page 83 *compatible* with a psychological explanation?

3

Compare the argument of this essay with Flint's comments on a Freudian reading of *Hamlet* (pages 63–64). What modifications does Selden make here to a traditional Freudian reading?

4

'Hamlet's word-play is the key to his unconscious' (last paragraph). Do you think Selden has demonstrated this in his essay?

Andrew Gurr

*Andrew Gurr is Professor of English
Literature at the University of Reading,
and author of numerous critical studies.*

ESSAY

Hamlet's claim to
the crown of Denmark

Shakespeare took some trouble to make it clear that his
Denmark had an elective system of kingship. The pompous
noises which Rosencrantz and Guildenstern make about the
disasters that follow the cease of majesty (III.3.15) should not
be allowed to conceal the consequences which elective kingship
has for any reading of the play. For one thing, it meant that
Hamlet was not justified in calling King Claudius a usurper on
the grounds that he himself was the rightful heir to his father's
crown. Nor should he have declared himself 'Hamlet the Dane',
that is, the rightful King of Denmark, as he does over Ophelia's
grave.

Kingship in Shakespeare's time was the only conceivable
form of government. Kings were the supreme judges and
lawgivers for their people, and while the law did prescribe fairly
tightly what kings were expected to do, their authority was so
great that there was no machinery to stop a king from misbe-
having. The office of king was clearly defined, and theoretically
its duties were invariable: fairly administering the law and
correcting wrongdoing. The personality which occupied that
office, however, was of course a completely variable thing, and
because most crowns passed by inheritance from father to son

there was little any people could do if the son turned out to be a bad personality. A good personality was more likely to make a good king than a bad one, of course. But under England's hereditary monarchy there was no machinery for choosing one possible king before another. That possibility did theoretically exist in kingdoms where the ruler was elected by the royal council. But even royal councils could be deceived by appearances, as they were in Denmark over King Claudius. Hamlet suffers under the greatest political uncertainty of his time: what to do about your country's government when your ruler is a criminal personality. He suffers that uncertainty in isolation because only he knows that the king Denmark has elected is a murderer.

The process of electing kings is mentioned several times in the play. The most open references are in Act V, as if we were expected by then to be sorting out some of the implications. In V.2.65 Hamlet includes in his catalogue of Claudius's crimes the fact that he 'Popped in between th'election and my hopes'. Hamlet had hoped to follow his father as King of Denmark, but Claudius was elected instead. Again in V.2.349–350 when Hamlet is dying he tries to settle Denmark's future government. Remembering the 'delicate and tender' prince whom he had seen go past on his way to slaughter twenty thousand Poles (IV.4.48, 60), he offers his posthumous vote. 'I do prophesy th'election lights/ On Fortinbras', he declares. 'He has *my* dying voice' (author's italics). Fortinbras had found himself in the same position as Hamlet before the play begins. Just as the old King Hamlet had been followed not by young Hamlet his son but by his brother Claudius, so old King Fortinbras had been followed by his brother, 'uncle of young Fortinbras' (I.2.28). In both Denmark and Norway the son had not succeeded his father to the throne. The dying Hamlet's attempt to secure the election for Fortinbras is perhaps designed as an oblique reward to the revenger who, unlike the other two revengers, Hamlet himself and Laertes, did not follow his revenge through.

Elective kingship was an older custom in Europe than kingship through succession and primogeniture, inheritance by the oldest son, which was the custom England followed in Shakespeare's time. In many medieval kingdoms a new king was elected by the council of the old king's closest advisers. England had an elective kingship until Edward I in 1272 changed the custom, and France was elective until 1270. In Shakespeare's time elective kingship was unusual, but in a century which delved deeply into the politics of kingship it was by no means a wholly strange custom. The opening of one of Shakespeare's earliest plays, *Titus Andronicus*, sets out the alternative ways of getting a new ruler, 'successive title' or election. Shakespeare had dealt with kingship by hereditary succession, with all its dynastic complications, at some length in the English history plays. Shortly before writing *Hamlet* he had turned back to Roman history, where there was no hereditary succession, and wrote a play, *Julius Caesar*, the central question of which is a rather dubious form of election. The citizens' offer of a crown to Caesar, which makes Brutus decide to assassinate him because of the danger he poses to Roman liberty, is a form of popular election. A version of this popular election process appears in *Hamlet* when Laertes returns to avenge his murdered father, and the mob cry 'Choose we! Laertes shall be king' (IV.5.108).

In *Hamlet* the elective kingship has a number of implications which would not have been clear immediately even to the first audiences at the play. Election was so rare and old-fashioned by 1600 that any audience would at first assume the kingship of Denmark to be hereditary. Indeed, there seems to be some deliberate confusing of the issue in the opening scenes. When Horatio and the soldiers meet the ghost of the dead King Hamlet in the first scene, for instance, they resolve to tell their story to 'young Hamlet'. This they will do 'As needful in our loves, fitting our duty' (I.1.174). Any normal Elizabethan would assume here that their primary duty is very properly to tell the dead king's son, who they would assume to be the new King Hamlet. Only when the second scene begins two lines later, and the new king speaks his first line about 'Hamlet our dear *brother*'s death' (author's italics) should we realise that the crown has not gone by hereditary succession to the dead king's son, but to his brother instead. An audience should therefore begin to feel uneasy in this second scene. Horatio and the soldiers have agreed that it is their duty to tell the Ghost's son, not the King, about their encounter. They have agreed that it is their duty not to tell the new king, but the king's nephew.

So, we should now ask, why should they avoid telling the new king? And why is young Hamlet not the new king?

At this point in the play there is nothing to tell us that Denmark's kingship is elective, and that therefore Claudius may be a rightful king. The case of Fortinbras in Norway offers a precedent of a sort, of course. We also get a hint later in the scene when Claudius makes his declaration that Hamlet has his vote for the next vacancy in the kingship: 'For let the world take note,/ You are the most immediate to our throne' (I.2.108–109). This is a resounding declaration, and one which is designed to leave Hamlet with no overt basis for resentment that he has been passed over for the kingship, especially if the kingship has been acquired correctly by election. It certainly confirms Hamlet's isolation from the rest of the court, an isolation already indicated by the fact that he is still wearing black clothes in mourning for his dead father while the rest of the court is colourfully dressed for the wedding of Claudius and Gertrude. Now Claudius has put him in his place as the King's chosen favourite. Hamlet's sulky refusal to be nice to the new king cannot be approved by those courtiers who have elected the new king. What Hamlet's following soliloquy makes clear is that he is upset not at Claudius usurping his title, but at what he sees as the disgusting speed of his mother's remarriage. If at this point we assume that Hamlet must have been the heir apparent to his father, in a kingdom where rule was by succession, we must wonder at his failure to voice that grievance. If we think the kingship might have been elective, we can see one reason among others why he has to speak his grievances only to himself, and why he allows his mother's conduct to dominate his thoughts rather than the conduct of his new step-father, the King. What we wonder still is why he does not voice his feeling that he should have been king, but we see the higher priority in his mind, and wonder about that.

The first clear hint that Denmark has an elective kingship comes in the next scene, when Laertes is lecturing Ophelia about holding Hamlet's attention off. Because he is 'subject to his birth', says Laertes, he may not choose a wife for himself, but be circumscribed 'Unto the voice and yielding of that body/ Whereof he is the head' (I.3.23–24). The 'voice' is an elective vote, later called 'the main voice of Denmark' (line 28). Despite that hint, the elective nature of the Danish constitution is not made absolutely clear until the final scene, at V.2.65, and we may well ask why it is left so obscure for so long.

Once we eventually do know that Denmark's kingdom is elective, several small details, unclear at their first expression, alter their shape and suggest different views about what is going on in Elsinore. When Hamlet calls Claudius a usurper, and talks of his frustrated ambition, he can be doing so not, or not only, out of resentment that his own claim to the crown has been ignored. Hamlet plays games with his fellow-students who are spying on him. He emphasises his thwarted ambition and tells them he is revengeful as well as very proud and ambitious, but disarms the honest admission of revengefulness by making them think he merely resents Claudius for being elected instead of himself. The audience is better placed than Rosencrantz and Guildenstern to realise that his real ambition now is to revenge his father by killing Claudius. Technically Claudius has not usurped young Hamlet's title, because in an elective kingdom anyone with royal blood had a chance of being elected. If Claudius has usurped anyone's title, it is that of old King Hamlet, by his act of murder. Young Hamlet's assertion that Claudius stole the crown like a cutpurse (III.4.100) is based on Claudius's crime, not Hamlet's thwarted ambition. Claudius is a thief because he stole the crown from King Hamlet, not young Hamlet.

So we come to the question why Hamlet, in full view of the royal court and the King himself, all gathered at Ophelia's graveside, should declare: 'This is I,/ Hamlet the Dane' (V.1.253–254). It is an unequivocal declaration that he is the King of Denmark. Claudius has emphasised his use of the title often enough, in his first scene for instance ('You cannot speak of reason to the Dane', 'No jocund health that Denmark drinks today' — I.2.44, 125). Now Hamlet is usurping the title to his face. It is a peculiar declaration in several ways. First, Hamlet himself has never, even in soliloquy, said that he feels himself to be the rightful king. His claims to thwarted ambition were laid in front of Rosencrantz and Guildenstern to serve as distractions from the main cause of Hamlet's upset. Secondly, it is an open declaration that he feels Claudius should not have the crown. In this respect he is developing the idea which is to crop up several times a little later on, that he wants to confront Claudius with his crimes openly, to face him honestly like an antagonist in a duel. He will not stab him in the back or pour poison into his ears as Claudius himself is used to doing. *The Mousetrap* has been his declaration to Claudius that he knows about King Hamlet's murder, and that he in turn will murder Claudius. He underlines the point by saying that the stage murderer is 'one Lucianus, *nephew* to the king' (III.2.253 — author's italics). The stage murder which the Players act out is not just an imitation of Claudius killing the King his brother, but a prophecy that young Hamlet will kill the King his uncle. At V.2.60–62 he tells Horatio that the deaths of Rosencrantz and Guildenstern are the consequence of their interfering in the duel between himself and Claudius:

> 'Tis dangerous when the baser nature comes
> Between the pass and fell incensèd points
> Of mighty opposites.

Hamlet and Claudius are the mighty opposites, duelling with swords which have fatal incensed points. Hamlet is foretelling the future again.

There is also a third reason for Hamlet to make his claim to the crown. It is a more concealed point, which only becomes clear when the scene is staged as it was originally, at Shakespeare's Globe playhouse. In V.1. the mourners from the court are gathered around the stage trapdoor in the centre of the stage platform, where the gravedigger has been working and throwing up the old skulls which so intrigue Hamlet. This trapdoor has been used once before in the play. When the Ghost disappears at I.5.91 after telling Hamlet the story of the murder, it uses the trapdoor to descend back to its purgatorial fires. Later it cries from under the stage (lines 149, 155, 161, 181). Traditionally the trapdoor gave access to hell. The stage cover or 'shadow' had the heavens painted on it. The earth was the stage platform beneath the heavens. Hell was the understage area. In plays like *Dr Faustus* by Christopher Marlowe, devils came up to the earth of the stage platform through the trap. It was the proper route for the Ghost's return to his purgatorial fires. In Act V it was also, ironically, the appropriate place for the burial of Ophelia, since her death was at best, according to the priest, 'doubtful', and probably a suicide, so that she would be damned to eternity in hell. An Elizabethan audience, watching Laertes quarrel with the priest over his sister's burial rites, would note the association of the grave with hell, and remember the Ghost's exit. When Hamlet leaps into the same place and cries 'This is I, Hamlet the Dane', he is standing in for his father. Like the Ghost, he has returned to curse the living. The young Hamlet appears as his dead father Hamlet the Dane.

On the face of it, Claudius is a very good king. He defends Denmark against the threat of Fortinbras's invasion by setting the armourers to work overtime, and putting sentries on the battlements. In the event, he stops Fortinbras by simply dropping a word in the ear of his uncle the King. He is rightly sceptical of Polonius when he claims that Hamlet has been driven mad for love of Ophelia. He sets spies to watch Hamlet, and quickly ships him out of the country when Hamlet's apparent madness makes him kill his beloved's father. And, more important than all these practical politics, he is a legitimate ruler, duly elected by Polonius and the rest of the king's councillors. On the outside he is a rightful ruler. What is rotten about the 'state' of his kingship is his lack of inner goodness as a man. He is a usurper, not of young Hamlet's title to the crown but of old Hamlet's life, crown and queen. So far as appearances go, he is a good and rightful king. So far as morality goes, he is 'That spirit upon whose weal depends and rests/ The lives of many' (III.3.14–15), as Rosencrantz obsequiously puts it. In Denmark that weal is diseased, and as a result many of the lives which depend on it are lost.

AFTERTHOUGHTS

1

What do you understand by 'an elective system of kingship' (opening paragraph)?

2

Are you convinced that 'This is I/ Hamlet the Dane' is 'an unequivocal declaration that he is King of Denmark' (page 96)? How does Devlin view the same line (page 104)?

3

Why does Hamlet give his dying vote to Fortinbras?

4

If *Hamlet* is a play about elected kingships, can its political concerns be of any relevance to citizens of a modern democracy?

Diana Devlin

Diana Devlin has taught extensively in schools and colleges in the UK and US, and is closely involved with the International Shakespeare Globe Centre. She has published numerous critical studies.

ESSAY

Has Hamlet changed at all, after his return from England?

When Hamlet finally kills his uncle, he does so in a scene of great confusion, with characters collapsing like ninepins, and it is easy to think that the death of Claudius is achieved only as part of the general chaos. But it is my purpose here to show that the killing of Claudius came about through Hamlet's careful judgement of the moment, and not just by luck or chance. I intend to show, too, that Hamlet achieved his revenge because of an important change in his state of mind after his return from England.

First of all, the killing itself. Although the events around it happen swiftly, it is still possible to see how *certain* Hamlet is in everything he does, especially in contrast to his previous attempts to avenge his father's death.

When the royal party enters for the duel (Act V, scene 2) Hamlet takes Laertes's hand and is at great pains to make peace with him. 'Sir,' he finishes:

> . . . in this audience
> Let my disclaiming from a purposed evil

> Free me so far in your most generous thoughts
> That I have shot my arrow o'er the house
> And hurt my brother.

(V.2.234–238)

With this handsome apology, Laertes's personal motive for fighting vigorously is undermined. He tells Hamlet he is 'satisfied in nature'. He is therefore left fighting only for his honour. But since he already knows his honour is compromised by the intrigue with Claudius, his motive is wellnigh evaporated. His next lines must be a little hollow:

> I do receive your offered love like love,
> And will not wrong it.

(lines 245–246)

'I embrace it freely', replies Hamlet, 'And will this brothers' wager frankly pay'. He has the upper hand and knows it. If the duel is fair play, then this frankness is simply in line with his brotherly feeling towards Laertes, and they fight as two noble opponents. But if there is, as he must suspect, some plot which Claudius has set in motion, then his own ironic 'frankness' will undermine Laertes, who is less experienced in dishonour than Claudius. It may not be just good luck or even greater swordsmanship that makes Hamlet score two hits so rapidly in the fight.

Wary of anything the King does, Hamlet refuses to drink, but is reassured by the fact that when Gertrude drinks, Claudius does nothing. Hamlet rallies Laertes to fight harder, which he does — for Hamlet does not score his third hit. Laertes then makes a surprise lunge at Hamlet, before the next bout has properly begun. Hamlet's suspicion that the fight is not fair is now confirmed. Nevertheless, he continues with it until he sees his mother faint. Except for Claudius, who dare not draw attention to the Queen's plight, Hamlet is in fact the first character to notice the faint — since all other eyes are on Laertes and himself. When Gertrude reveals that the drink is poisoned, Hamlet's words and actions are swift, authoritative and reasonable:

> O, villainy! Ho! Let the door be locked.
> Treachery! Seek it out.

(lines 305–306)

While he must guess at once who the villain is, he does not strike as wildly as he did in the scene in his mother's bedroom, when he killed Polonius unnecessarily. He simply takes the logical step of having the doors locked to prevent escape. Laertes then confesses the true situation — explaining that both he and Hamlet are poisoned by the sword, that Gertrude is poisoned too, and that 'The King's to blame'. At last Claudius's guilt is fully exposed. In a split second, Hamlet recognises the moment of revenge and seizes it:

> The point envenomed too?
> Then, venom, to thy work.

(lines 315–316)

He wounds the King, but the courtiers — not as swift as he to comprehend the situation — call out 'Treason!', prompting the King to call on them to defend him.

At that moment, Hamlet has only Laertes's word that the sword is poisoned and that the two of them and Claudius will therefore die within half an hour. Leaving nothing to chance that he can possibly do something about, he takes the drink which he *knows* is poisoned — since he has just seen his mother die from it — and forces it down Claudius's throat before any of the courtiers can defend their king. The three adjectives that he speaks as he does it, 'incestuous, murderous, damnèd', bring together all the reasons he has for killing Claudius, and complete his act of just revenge.

Neither of the weapons with which Hamlet kills Claudius was prepared by him. Nor has he killed by any premeditated plan. But he has recognised the opportunity when it came, and seized it. For the first time his purpose has coincided with the circumstances and he has acted decisively. And my argument is that he has been moving towards this moment ever since his return from England. Let us now examine the evidence in the last Act which shows his changed state of mind, and the significance that Shakespeare seems to place on it.

From the moment the Ghost reveals himself in the first Act, we have seen Hamlet busy with words and deeds in pursuit of avenging his father, but always distracted from actually carrying out the revenge. His preoccupation with his mother's hasty marriage and his own self-contempt at not carrying out his purpose are the chief obstacles in his way, leading to violent behaviour towards Ophelia and his mother, to an interlude where he devotes himself to putting on a play about the murder, to a lost opportunity to kill the King that is swiftly followed by a reckless attempt (which in fact kills Polonius, and gives Claudius an excuse to get him transported away from Denmark altogether!), and to tortured soliloquies of self-reproach.

'The time is out of joint,' he complains just after meeting the Ghost:

> O cursèd spite,
> That ever I was born to set it right!
>
> (I.5.188–189)

This sense that time is not on his side remains with him right through to his departure for England. In his soliloquy then, having seen Fortinbras march purposefully off to fight for 'a little patch of ground/ That hath in it no profit but the name,' he makes several references to time and to his inability to fit thought and deed together in one action. ('Suit the action to the word, the word to the action,' he told the First Player, and yet he has been unable to do this himself.) He wonders if he is thinking too little or too much to be able to do what he believes he should be doing:

> Now, whether it be
> Bestial oblivion, or some craven scruple
> Of thinking too precisely on th'event —
> . . .
> — I do not know
> Why yet I live to say 'This thing's to do'
>
> (IV.4.39–44)

The audience, too, must feel frustrated that Hamlet has done so much planning and acting, but neither accomplished his revenge nor decided against doing so.

Hamlet's absence from Denmark fills only one scene of the play (Act IV, scene 5), when we see Ophelia's madness and Laertes's return to avenge his father, and then his sister too. News of Hamlet's return comes in the form of a letter to Horatio, delivered in Act IV, scene 6. In it, he briefly describes the battle in which he was taken prisoner by pirates:

They have dealt with me like thieves of mercy. But they knew
what they did. I am to do a good turn for them.

(IV.6.19–21)

This encounter is the first successful and balanced transaction
that Hamlet has had with anyone since the play began. We do
not know what bargain was struck, but clearly it satisfied both
sides and involved no trickery between them.

Hamlet's meeting with Horatio takes him, for no explained
reason, through the burial ground where Ophelia's grave is
being prepared, and he encounters the native wit of the First
Clown who is digging it. The exchange here, verbal this time,
is equally happy for Hamlet, a light-hearted banter on the
subject of death, which comes straight after his own life has
been endangered. But his reverie on mortality is cut short by
the entrance of Ophelia's funeral procession.

Hamlet's behaviour here at the grave is in some ways a
return to the hysterical, out-of-key performance he has given to
the court before. He rants and over-reacts to Laertes's grief,
deserving the accusations of madness he gets from both the King
and the Queen. But three features of the scene point towards a
new openness in his behaviour.

One is his full acknowledgement of his own identity. 'This
is I,/ Hamlet the Dane,' he announces (V.1.253–254), as if
owning himself fully for the first time. Another is the first
honest expression of his feeling for Ophelia. True, it comes out
as anger, overblown grief and resentment now, but that is
because it has been pent up for so long. The third is the scorn
for Laertes's sorrow being manifested in whining and showy
lamentation. 'What wilt thou do for her?' he asks (line 267),
''Swounds, show me what thou't do' (line 270). He seems to see
in Laertes a reflection of his own tendency towards self-pity:

> Nay, an thou'lt mouth,
> I'll rant as well as thou.

(V.1.279–280)

For the first time, Hamlet sees in someone else the weakness
of show and words, a sign that he himself is on his way to
conquering that same tendency. Later, he expresses regret to
Horatio at having been so wild:

But sure the bravery of his grief did put me
Into a towering passion.

(V.2.79–80)

At last he is alone with Horatio, telling him the story of the voyage and sea-fight. Only in retrospect will the audience note that after his departure to England Hamlet is never alone again, and therefore speaks no further soliloquies. The fighting inside his head has been replaced with real fighting. The transition is marked at the lines to Horatio:

Sir, in my heart there was a kind of fighting
That would not let me sleep.

(V.2.4–5)

Whatever that mental conflict was, it prompted him to search for the papers Rosencrantz and Guildenstern were carrying, and so discover the plot to have him executed in England. This was the first time Hamlet acted impulsively and it paid off. For the first time, the 'occasion' did not 'inform against' him. He worked on a hunch that something was amiss, and so saved his own life. He learned that to trust his own actions might sometimes be better than to trust his thoughts:

Our indiscretion sometimes serves us well
When our deep plots do pall

(line 8)

He draws from this a new conclusion that relieves him of such heavy responsibility for his own fate:

There's a divinity that shapes our ends,
Rough-hew them how we will

(lines 10–11)

The account to Horatio has been delayed by the scene at Ophelia's grave. Hamlet's philosophical remark therefore comes after his contemplation of mortality over Yorick's skull. Reflection is now coming *after* action for Hamlet, letting him recognise that his thoughts are not in charge of his life.

Having described the uncovering of the plot, Hamlet goes on to tell Horatio of the counter-plot that condemned Rosencrantz and Guildenstern to the fate that was planned for him.

His explanation reveals a necessary and expedient ruthlessness, and places him for the first time on equal footing with Claudius:

> 'Tis dangerous when the baser nature comes
> Between the pass and fell incensèd points
> Of mighty opposites.

(lines 60–62)

He is no longer whining boyishly, or protesting at the 'cursèd spite' that burdened him with an intolerable duty. Instead, he is wearing that duty as his rightful possession. Even Horatio is surprised at this decisiveness, exclaiming 'Why, what a king is this!'

Though not a king, he does speak as a mature man, and as heir to the throne of Denmark, expressing his purpose towards Claudius boldly in his own terms instead of in his father's:

> He that hath killed my King and whored my mother,
> Popped in between th'election and my hopes,
> Thrown out his angle for my proper life,
> And with such cozenage — is't not perfect conscience
> To quit him with this arm? And is't not to be damned
> To let this canker of our nature come
> In further evil?

(lines 64–70)

When Horatio points out that news of Hamlet's counter-plot will soon reach Claudius, Hamlet's confidence is not to be shaken. 'The interim is mine,' he says, no longer at odds with time.

The attitude which Hamlet brings to the final scene of the play is this, then: Claudius has done wrong to his father, his mother, himself, the country and human nature. Hamlet now knows himself to be a 'mighty opposite' who will let nothing stand in the way of his revenge. He knows that his opportune time is short, but he also knows that length of time is irrelevant to any man's life, his own or Claudius's. He has learned that 'deep plots' may not be as effective as an occasional rashness or indiscretion. He needs not to invent an opportunity to kill Claudius, but to be ready for it when it comes.

Osric comes on to offer the wager. Hamlet accepts it for all its obvious danger. He is asked if he wants to delay the fight with Laertes. His answer — superficially a polite reply to the

King — is an ironic confirmation that he will be alert to any move, and ready to act on it:

> I am constant to my purposes. They follow the King's pleasure. If his fitness speaks, mine is ready, now or whensoever, provided I be so able as now.
>
> (lines 195–197)

If the wager were above-board, Hamlet stands a good chance of winning. He assures Horatio that he has been in constant practice and will win at the odds. 'But', he continues:

> ... thou wouldst not think how ill all's here about my heart.
>
> (lines 206–207)

It sounds like the same sort of apprehensive feeling he had on the ship, the feeling that prompted him to steal the packet of letters. Horatio suggests that he should listen to the fear, and put off the duel. But Hamlet insists on going through with it. 'We defy augury,' he says (line 213).

The usual way to 'defy augury' is to scorn it, to dismiss it contemptuously. Hamlet's attitude is a little different. He does not reject the significance of his intuition, or seek a consoling interpretation for his uneasiness (as Julius Caesar does when he dreams a fearful dream in *Julius Caesar*, Act II, scene 2). Instead, Hamlet goes forward with a clear purpose, to use this 'interim' to the best advantage, but with a clear premonition that he might die:

> There is special providence in the fall of a sparrow. If it be now, 'tis not to come. If it be not to come, it will be now. If it be not now, yet it will come. The readiness is all. Since no man knows of aught he leaves, what is't to leave betimes? Let be.
>
> (lines 213–218)

The exquisite balance of the prose here forewarns us, I think, of what will happen: Hamlet will fulfil his purpose, and he will die while doing it. Its serene tone is a strong hint that Hamlet too believes this, and accepts it.

Claudius dies, then, because Hamlet is ready and waiting to kill him. Not waiting in stillness, but waiting and fighting.

AFTERTHOUGHTS

1

Compare this essay with Gardiner's account of Hamlet's behaviour in the final Act of the play (pages 32–33).

2

Compare Devlin's view of the line 'This is I,/ Hamlet the Dane' (page 104) with Gurr's interpretation (page 96).

3

What arguments are advanced in this essay to support the case made in its opening paragraph? Are you convinced?

4

Devlin comments on the 'serene tone' of the speech she quotes in the penultimate paragraph of her essay. Do you agree with her assessment of it?

A PRACTICAL GUIDE TO ESSAY WRITING

INTRODUCTION

First, a word of warning. Good essays are the product of a creative engagement with literature. So never try to restrict your studies to what you think will be 'useful in the exam'. Ironically, you will restrict your grade potential if you do.

This doesn't mean, of course, that you should ignore the basic skills of essay writing. When you read critics, make a conscious effort to notice *how* they communicate their ideas. The guidelines that follow offer advice of a more explicit kind. But they are no substitute for practical experience. It is never easy to express ideas with clarity and precision. But the more often you tackle the problems involved and experiment to find your own voice, the more fluent you will become. So practise writing essays as often as possible.

HOW TO PLAN
AN ESSAY

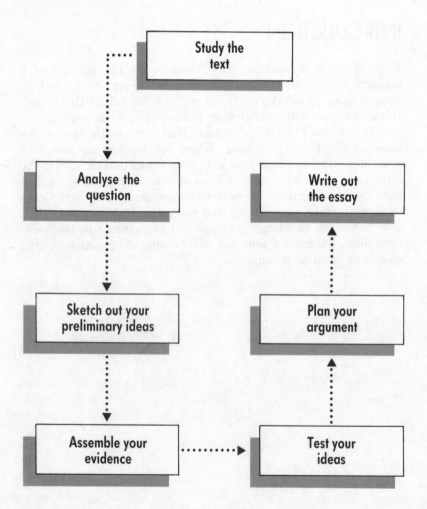

Study the
text

Analyse the
question

Write out
the essay

Sketch out your
preliminary ideas

Plan your
argument

Assemble your
evidence

Test your
ideas

Study the text

The first step in writing a good essay is to get to know the set text well. Never write about a text until you are fully familiar with it. Even a discussion of the opening chapter of a novel, for example, should be informed by an understanding of the book as a whole. Literary texts, however, are by their very nature complex and on a first reading you are bound to miss many significant features. Re-read the book with care, if possible more than once. Look up any unfamiliar words in a good dictionary and if the text you are studying was written more than a few decades ago, consult the *Oxford English Dictionary* to find out whether the meanings of any terms have shifted in the intervening period.

Good books are difficult to put down when you first read them. But a more leisurely second or third reading gives you the opportunity to make notes on those features you find significant. An index of characters and events is often useful, particularly when studying novels with a complex plot or time scheme. The main aim, however, should be to record your *responses* to the text. By all means note, for example, striking images. But be sure to add *why* you think them striking. Similarly, record any thoughts you may have on interesting comparisons with other texts, puzzling points of characterisation, even what you take to be aesthetic blemishes. The important thing is to annotate fully and adventurously. The most seemingly idiosyncratic comment may later lead to a crucial area of discussion which you would otherwise have overlooked. It helps to have a working copy of the text in which to mark up key passages and jot down marginal comments (although obviously these practices are taboo when working with library, borrowed or valuable copies!). But keep a fuller set of notes as well and organise these under appropriate headings.

Literature does not exist in an aesthetic vacuum, however, and you should try to find out as much as possible about the context of its production and reception. It is particularly important to read other works by the same author and writings by contemporaries. At this early stage, you may want to restrict your secondary reading to those standard reference works, such as biographies, which are widely available in public libraries. In the long run, however, it pays to read as wide a range of critical studies as possible.

Some students, and tutors, worry that such studies may stifle the development of any truly personal response. But this won't happen if you are alert to the danger and read critically. After all, you wouldn't passively accept what a stranger told you in conversation. The fact that a critic's views are in print does not necessarily make them any more authoritative (as a glance at the review pages of the *TLS* and *London Review of Books* will reveal). So question the views you find: 'Does this critic's interpretation agree with mine and where do we part company?' 'Can it be right to try and restrict this text's meanings to those found by its author or first audience?' 'Doesn't this passage treat a theatrical text as though it were a novel?' Often it is views which you reject which prove most valuable since they challenge you to articulate your own position with greater clarity. Be sure to keep careful notes on what the critic wrote, and your *reactions* to what the critic wrote.

Analyse the question

You cannot begin to answer a question until you understand what task it is you have been asked to perform. Recast the question in your own words and reconstruct the line of reasoning which lies behind it. Where there is a choice of topics, try to choose the one for which you are best prepared. It would, for example, be unwise to tackle 'How far do you agree that in *Paradise Lost* Milton transformed the epic models he inherited from ancient Greece and Rome?' without a working knowledge of Homer and Virgil (or *Paradise Lost* for that matter!). If you do not already know the works of these authors, the question should spur you on to read more widely — or discourage you from attempting it at all. The scope of an essay, however, is not always so obvious and you must remain alert to the implied demands of each question. How could you possibly 'Consider the view that *Wuthering Heights* transcends the conventions of the Gothic novel' without reference to at least some of those works which, the question suggests, have *not* transcended Gothic conventions?

When you have decided on a topic, analyse the terms of the question itself. Sometimes these self-evidently require careful definition: *tragedy* and *irony*, for example, are notoriously difficult concepts to pin down and you will probably need to consult a good dictionary of literary terms. Don't ignore, however, those seemingly innocuous phrases which often smuggle in significant assumptions. 'Does Macbeth lack the nobility of the true tragic hero?' obviously invites you to discuss nobility and the nature of the tragic hero. But what of 'lack' and 'true' — do they suggest that the play would be improved had Shakespeare depicted Macbeth in a different manner? or that tragedy is superior to other forms of drama? Remember that you are not expected meekly to agree with the assumptions implicit in the question. Some questions are deliberately provocative in order to stimulate an engaged response. Don't be afraid to take up the challenge.

Sketch out your preliminary ideas

'Which comes first, the evidence or the answer?' is one of those chicken and egg questions. How can you form a view without inspecting the evidence? But how can you know which evidence is relevant without some idea of what it is you are looking for? In practice the mind reviews evidence and formulates preliminary theories or hypotheses at one and the same time, although for the sake of clarity we have separated out the processes. Remember that these early ideas are only there to get you started. You *expect* to modify them in the light of the evidence you uncover. Your initial hypothesis may be an instinctive 'gut-reaction'. Or you may find that you prefer to 'sleep on the problem', allowing ideas to gell over a period of time. Don't worry in either case. The mind is quite capable of processing a vast amount of accumulated evidence, the product of previous reading and thought, and reaching sophisticated intuitive judgements. Eventually, however, you are going to have to think carefully through any ideas you arrive at by such intuitive processes. Are they logical? Do they take account of all the relevant factors? Do they fully answer the question set? Are there any obvious reasons to qualify or abandon them?

Assemble your evidence

Now is the time to return to the text and re-read it with the question and your working hypothesis firmly in mind. Many of the notes you have already made are likely to be useful, but assess the precise relevance of this material and make notes on any new evidence you discover. The important thing is to cast your net widely and take into account points which tend to undermine your case as well as those that support it. As always, ensure that your notes are full, accurate, and reflect your own critical judgements.

You may well need to go outside the text if you are to do full justice to the question. If you think that the 'Oedipus complex' may be relevant to an answer on *Hamlet* then read Freud and a balanced selection of those critics who have discussed the appropriateness of applying psychoanalytical theories to the interpretation of literature. Their views can most easily be tracked down by consulting the annotated bibliographies held by most major libraries (and don't be afraid to ask a librarian for help in finding and using these). Remember that you go to works of criticism not only to obtain information but to stimulate you into clarifying your own position. And that since life is short and many critical studies are long, judicious use of a book's index and/or contents list is not to be scorned. You can save yourself a great deal of future labour if you carefully record full bibliographic details at this stage.

Once you have collected the evidence, organise it coherently. Sort the detailed points into related groups and identify the quotations which support these. You must also assess the relative importance of each point, for in an essay of limited length it is essential to establish a firm set of priorities, exploring some ideas in depth while discarding or subordinating others.

Test your ideas

As we stressed earlier, a hypothesis is only a proposal, and one that you fully expect to modify. Review it with the evidence before you. Do you really still believe in it? It would be surprising if you did not want to modify it in some way. If you cannot see any problems, others may. Try discussing your ideas with friends and relatives. Raise them in class discussions. Your tutor is certain to welcome your initiative. The critical process is essentially collaborative and there is absolutely no reason why you should not listen to and benefit from the views of others. Similarly, you should feel free to test your ideas against the theories put forward in academic journals and books. But do not just borrow what you find. Critically analyse the views on offer and, where appropriate, integrate them into your own pattern of thought. You must, of course, give full acknowledgement to the sources of such views.

Do not despair if you find you have to abandon or modify significantly your initial position. The fact that you are prepared to do so is a mark of intellectual integrity. Dogmatism is never an academic virtue and many of the best essays explore the *process* of scholarly enquiry rather than simply record its results.

Plan your argument

Once you have more or less decided on your attitude to the question (for an answer is never really 'finalised') you have to present your case in the most persuasive manner. In order to do this you must avoid meandering from point to point and instead produce an organised argument — a structured flow of ideas and supporting evidence, leading logically to a conclusion which fully answers the question. Never begin to write until you have produced an outline of your argument.

You may find it easiest to begin by sketching out its main stage as a flow chart or some other form of visual presentation. But eventually you should produce a list of paragraph topics. The paragraph is the conventional written demarcation for a unit of thought and you can outline an argument quite simply by briefly summarising the substance of each paragraph and then checking that these points (you may remember your English teacher referring to them as topic sentences) really do follow a coherent order. Later you will be able to elaborate on each topic, illustrating and qualifying it as you go along. But you will find this far easier to do if you possess from the outset a clear map of where you are heading.

All questions require some form of an argument. Even so-called 'descriptive' questions *imply* the need for an argument. An adequate answer to the request to 'Outline the role of Iago in *Othello*' would do far more than simply list his appearances on stage. It would at the very least attempt to provide some *explanation* for his actions — is he, for example, a representative stage 'Machiavel'? an example of pure evil, 'motiveless malignity'? or a realistic study of a tormented personality reacting to identifiable social and psychological pressures?

Your conclusion ought to address the terms of the question. It may seem obvious, but 'how far do you agree', 'evaluate', 'consider', 'discuss', etc, are *not* interchangeable formulas and your conclusion must take account of the precise wording of the question. If asked 'How far do you agree?', the concluding paragraph of your essay really should state whether you are in complete agreement, total disagreement, or, more likely, partial agreement. Each preceding paragraph should have a clear justification for its existence and help to clarify the reasoning which underlies your conclusion. If you find that a paragraph serves no good purpose (perhaps merely summarising the plot), do not hesitate to discard it.

The arrangement of the paragraphs, the overall strategy of the argument, can vary. One possible pattern is dialectical: present the arguments in favour of one point of view (**thesis**); then turn to counter-arguments or to a rival interpretation (**antithesis**); finally evaluate the competing claims and arrive at your own conclusion (**synthesis**). You may, on the other hand, feel so convinced of the merits of one particular case that you wish to devote your entire essay to arguing that viewpoint persuasively (although it is always desirable to indicate, however briefly, that you are aware of alternative, if flawed, positions). As the essays contained in this volume demonstrate, there are many other possible strategies. Try to adopt the one which will most comfortably accommodate the demands of the question and allow you to express your thoughts with the greatest possible clarity.

Be careful, however, not to apply abstract formulas in a mechanical manner. It is true that you should be careful to define your terms. It is *not* true that every essay should begin with 'The dictionary defines x as ...'. In fact, definitions are often best left until an appropriate moment for their introduction arrives. Similarly every essay should have a beginning, middle and end. But it does not follow that in your opening paragraph you should announce an intention to write an essay, or that in your concluding paragraph you need to signal an imminent desire to put down your pen. The old adages are often useful reminders of what constitutes good practice, but they must be interpreted intelligently.

Write out the essay

Once you have developed a coherent argument you should aim to communicate it in the most effective manner possible. Make certain you clearly identify yourself, and the question you are answering. Ideally, type your answer, or at least ensure your handwriting is legible and that you leave sufficient space for your tutor's comments. Careless presentation merely distracts from the force of your argument. Errors of grammar, syntax and spelling are far more serious. At best they are an irritating blemish, particularly in the work of a student who should be sensitive to the nuances of language. At worst, they seriously confuse the sense of your argument. If you are aware that you have stylistic problems of this kind, ask your tutor for advice at the earliest opportunity. Everyone, however, is liable to commit the occasional howler. The only remedy is to give yourself plenty of time in which to proof-read your manuscript (often reading it aloud is helpful) before submitting it.

Language, however, is not only an instrument of communication; it is also an instrument of thought. If you want to think clearly and precisely you should strive for a clear, precise prose style. Keep your sentences short and direct. Use modern, straightforward English wherever possible. Avoid repetition, clichés and wordiness. Beware of generalisations, simplifications, and overstatements. Orwell analysed the relationship between stylistic vice and muddled thought in his essay 'Politics and the English Language' (1946) — it remains essential reading (and is still readily available in volume 4 of the Penguin *Collected Essays, Journalism and Letters*). Generalisations, for example, are always dangerous. They are rarely true and tend to suppress the individuality of the texts in question. A remark such as 'Keats always employs sensuous language in his poetry' is not only fatuous (what, after all, does it mean? is *every* word he wrote equally 'sensuous'?) but tends to obscure interesting distinctions which could otherwise be made between, say, the descriptions in the 'Ode on a Grecian Urn' and those in 'To Autumn'.

The intelligent use of quotations can help you make your points with greater clarity. Don't sprinkle them throughout your essay without good reason. There is no need, for example, to use them to support uncontentious statements of fact. 'Macbeth murdered Duncan' does not require textual evidence (unless you wish to dispute Thurber's brilliant parody, 'The Great Macbeth Murder Mystery', which reveals Lady Macbeth's father as the culprit!). Quotations should be included, however, when they are necessary to support your case. The proposition that Macbeth's imaginative powers wither after he has killed his king would certainly require extensive quotation: you would almost certainly want to analyse key passages from both before and after the murder (perhaps his first and last soliloquies?). The key word here is 'analyse'. Quotations cannot make your points on their own. It is up to you to demonstrate their relevance and clearly explain to your readers *why* you want them to focus on the passage you have selected.

Most of the academic conventions which govern the presentation of essays are set out briefly in the style sheet below. The question of gender, however, requires fuller discussion. More than half the population of the world is female. Yet many writers still refer to an undifferentiated *man*kind. Or write of the author and *his* public. We do not think that this convention has much to recommend it. At the very least, it runs the risk of introducing unintended sexist attitudes. And at times leads to such patent absurdities as 'Cleopatra's final speech asserts *man*'s true nobility'. With a little thought, you can normally find ways of expressing yourself which do not suggest that the typical author, critic or reader is male. Often you can simply use plural forms, which is probably a more elegant solution than relying on such awkward formulations as 's/he' or 'he and she'. You should also try to avoid distinguishing between male and female authors on the basis of forenames. Why *Jane* Austen and not *George* Byron? Refer to all authors by their last names unless there is some good reason not to. Where there may otherwise be confusion, say between T S and George Eliot, give the name in full when it first occurs and thereafter use the last name only.

Finally, keep your audience firmly in mind. Tutors and examiners are interested in understanding your conclusions and the processes by which you arrived at them. They are not interested in reading a potted version of a book they already know. **So don't pad out your work with plot summary.**

Hints for examinations

In an examination you should go through exactly the same processes as you would for the preparation of a term essay. The only difference lies in the fact that some of the stages will have had to take place before you enter the examination room. This should not bother you unduly. Examiners are bound to avoid the merely eccentric when they come to formulate papers and if you have read widely and thought deeply about the central issues raised by your set texts you can be confident you will have sufficient material to answer the majority of questions sensibly.

The fact that examinations impose strict time limits makes it *more* rather than less, important that you plan carefully. There really is no point in floundering into an answer without any idea of where you are going, particularly when there will not be time to recover from the initial error.

Before you begin to answer any question at all, study the entire paper with care. Check that you understand the rubric and know how many questions you have to answer and whether any are compulsory. It may be comforting to spot a title you feel confident of answering well, but don't rush to tackle it: read *all* the questions before deciding which *combination* will allow you to display your abilities to the fullest advantage. Once you have made your choice, analyse each question, sketch out your ideas, assemble the evidence, review your initial hypothesis, play your argument, *before* trying to write out an answer. And make notes at each stage: not only will these help you arrive at a sensible conclusion, but examiners are impressed by evidence of careful thought.

Plan your time as well as your answers. If you have practised writing timed essays as part of your revision, you should not find this too difficult. There can be a temptation to allocate extra time to the questions you know you can answer well; but this is always a short-sighted policy. You will find yourself left to face a question which would in any event have given you difficulty without even the time to give it serious thought. It is, moreover, easier to gain marks at the lower end of the scale than at the upper, and you will never compensate for one poor answer by further polishing two satisfactory answers. Try to leave some time at the end of the examination to re-read your answers and correct any obvious errors. If the worst comes to the worst and you run short of time, don't just keep writing until you are forced to break off in mid-paragraph. It is far better to provide for the examiner a set of notes which indicate the overall direction of your argument.

Good luck — but if you prepare for the examination conscientiously and tackle the paper in a methodical manner, you won't need it!

Line references should normally be given in assignment essays and in examination essays where a text is supplied.

ities (III.1.158) alerts us to the equation which is made throughout the play between sanity and fitness to rule. Hamlet's disorder not only transgresses acceptable aristocratic behaviour but can be spoken of as something threatening the well-being of the state as well as of the individual. Ophelia's own affliction provides a useful point of contrast with the Prince. When she has broken down, in IV.5, her songs and speech have an internal logic, revealed through her obsession with abandoned maids, false love, and memory. 'A document in madness: thoughts and remembrance fitted' (IV.5.179–180), comments Laertes on her pointed distribution of flowers and herbs. Yet, self-enclosed, her words lack those connections with other protagonists which would involve and endanger anyone but herself: 'poor Ophelia' excites compassion, not personal anxiety. On the other hand, Claudius observing Hamlet remarks, with concern for his own position, that 'what he spake, though it lacked form a little,/ Was not like madness. There's something in his soul/ O'er which his melancholy sits on brood' (III.1.164–166).

short verse quotation incorporated in the text of the essay, within quotation marks. Line endings are indicated by a slash (/).

Deviance from a behavioural norm was frequently, in the Renaissance period, described in physical terms, as the over-ponderance of a 'humour' or 'complexion' — of blood, choler, melancholy or phlegm — in the body-state's defensive mechanism: the 'o'ergrowth of some complexion,/ Oft breaking down the pales and forts of reason' (I.4.27–28). Shakespeare's audience, like Claudius, would have had little trouble in identifying as the attributes of melancholy, the peculiarities which, regulated or involuntary fashion, set Hamlet apart.

Timothy Bright's *Treatise of Melancholy* (1586), a possible if not provable influence on Shakespeare, provides ready evidence of how this fashionable malady could be recognised:

book title in italics. In a handwritten or typed manuscript this would appear as underlining: Treatise of Melancholy.

Three dots (ellipsis) indicate where words or phrases have been cut from a quotation.

> The perturbations of melancholy are for the most part sad and fearful . . . as distrust, doubt, diffidence, or despair, sometimes furious, and sometimes merry in appearance, through a kind of Sardonian [sardonic], and false laughter, as the humour is disposed that procureth these diversions.

Hamlet bids the court, and us, to be wary of his initial display of mourning. His trappings and suits of woe, his sighs and his 'dejected 'haviour of the visage' (I.2.81) are enumerated by him

long prose quotation indented and introduced by a colon. Quotation marks are not needed.

62

We have divided the following information into two sections. Part A describes those rules which it is essential to master no matter what kind of essay you are writing (including examination answers). Part B sets out some of the more detailed conventions which govern the documentation of essays.

PART A: LAYOUT

Titles of texts

Titles of published books, plays (of any length), long poems, pamphlets and periodicals (including newspapers and magazines), works of classical literature, and films should be underlined: e.g. David Copperfield (novel), Twelfth Night (play), Paradise Lost (long poem), Critical Quarterly (periodical), Horace's Ars Poetica (Classical work), Apocalypse Now (film).

Notice how important it is to distinguish between titles and other names. Hamlet is the play; Hamlet the prince. Wuthering Heights is the novel; Wuthering Heights the house. Underlining is the equivalent in handwritten or typed manuscripts of printed italics. So what normally appears in this volume as *Othello* would be written as Othello in your essay.

Titles of articles, essays, short stories, short poems, songs, chapters of books, speeches, and newspaper articles are enclosed in quotation marks; e.g. 'The Flea' (short poem), 'The Prussian Officer' (short story), 'Middleton's Chess Strategies' (article), 'Thatcher Defects!' (newspaper headline).

Exceptions: Underlining titles or placing them within quotation marks does not apply to sacred writings (e.g. Bible, Koran, Old Testament, Gospels) or parts of a book (e.g. Preface, Introduction, Appendix).

It is generally incorrect to place quotation marks around a title of a published book which you have underlined. The exception is 'titles within titles': e.g. 'Vanity Fair': A Critical Study (title of a book about *Vanity Fair*).

Quotations

Short verse quotations of a single line or part of a line should be incorporated within quotation marks as part of the running text of your essay. Quotations of two or three lines of verse are treated in the same way, with line endings indicated by a slash(/). For example:

1   In <u>Julius Caesar</u>, Antony says of Brutus, 'This was the noblest Roman of them all'.
2   The opening of Antony's famous funeral oration, 'Friends, Romans, Countrymen, lend me your ears;/ I come to bury Caesar not to praise him', is a carefully controlled piece of rhetoric.

Longer verse quotations of more than three lines should be indented from the main body of the text and introduced in most cases with a colon. Do not enclose indented quotations within quotation marks. For example:

It is worth pausing to consider the reasons Brutus gives to justify his decision to assassinate Caesar:

> It must be by his death; and for my part,
> I know no personal cause to spurn at him,
> But for the general. He would be crowned.
> How might that change his nature, there's the question.

At first glance his rationale may appear logical . . .

Prose quotations of less than three lines should be incorporated in the text of the essay, within quotation marks. Longer prose quotations should be indented and the quotation marks omitted. For example:

1   Before his downfall, Caesar rules with an iron hand. His political opponents, the Tribunes Marullus and Flavius, are 'put to silence' for the trivial offence of 'pulling scarfs off Caesar's image'.
2   It is interesting to note the rhetorical structure of Brutus's Forum speech:

> Romans, countrymen, and lovers, hear me for my cause, and be silent that you may hear. Believe me for my honour, and have respect to mine honour that you may believe. Censure me in your wisdom, and awake your senses, that you may the better judge.

Tenses: When you are relating the events that occur within a work of fiction, or describing the author's technique, it is the convention to use the present tense. Even though Orwell published *Animal Farm* in 1945, the book *describes* the animals' seizure of Manor Farm. Similarly, Macbeth always *murders* Duncan, despite the passage of time.

PART B: DOCUMENTATION

When quoting from verse of more than twenty lines, provide line references: e.g. In 'Upon Appleton House' Marvell's mower moves 'With whistling scythe and elbow strong' (l.393).

Quotations from plays should be identified by act, scene and line references: e.g. Prospero, in Shakespeare's The Tempest, refers to Caliban as 'A devil, a born devil' (IV.1.188). (i.e. Act 4. Scene 1. Line 188).

Quotations from prose works should provide a chapter reference and, where appropriate, a page reference.

Bibliographies should list full details of all sources consulted. The way is which they are presented varies, but one standard format is as follows:

1 Books and articles are listed in alphabetical order by the author's last name. Initials are placed after the surname.
2 If you are referring to a chapter or article within a larger work, you list it by reference to the author of the article or chapter, not the editor (although the editor is also named in the reference).
3 Give (in parentheses) the place and date of publication, e.g. (London, 1962). These details can be found within the book itself. Here are some examples:

> Brockbank, J. P., 'Shakespeare's Histories, English and Roman', in Ricks, C. (ed.) English Drama to 1710 (Sphere History of Literature in the English Language) (London, 1971).
>
> Gurr, A., 'Richard III and the Democratic Process', Essays in Criticism 24 (1974), pp. 39–47.
>
> Spivack, B., Shakespeare and the Allegory of Evil (New York, 1958).

Footnotes: In general, try to avoid using footnotes and build your references into the body of the essay wherever possible. When you do use them give the full bibliographic reference to a work in the first instance and then use a short title: e.g. See K. Smidt, <u>Unconformities in Shakespeare's History Plays</u> (London, 1982), pp. 43–47 becomes Smidt (pp. 43–47) thereafter. Do not use terms such as 'ibid.' or 'op. cit.' unless you are absolutely sure of their meaning.

There is a principle behind all this seeming pedantry. The reader ought to be able to find and check your references and quotations as quickly and easily as possible. Give additional information, such as canto or volume number whenever you think it will assist your reader.

SUGGESTIONS FOR FURTHER READING

Texts

The following editions offer particularly stimulating Introductions:

Hibbard, G R (ed.), *Hamlet* (Oxford Shakespeare; Oxford, 1987)

Jenkins, H (ed.), *Hamlet* (new Arden Shakespeare; London, 1982)

Spencer, T J B (ed.), *Hamlet* (New Penguin Shakespeare; Harmondsworth, 1980)

General studies (containing substantial discussions of *Hamlet*)

Barton, A, 'Shakespeare: His Tragedies', in C Ricks (ed.), *English Drama to 1710* (Sphere History of Literature in the English Language; London, 1971)

Bradley, A C, *Shakespearean Tragedy* (London, 1904)

Dollimore, J, *Radical Tragedy* (Brighton, 1984)

Holloway, J (ed.), *The Story of the Night* (London, 1961)

Reynolds, P, *Text into Performance* (Harmondsworth, 1986)

Frye, N, *Fools of Time: Studies in Shakespearean Tragedy* (Toronto, 1967)

Wells, S (ed.), *The Cambridge Companion To Shakespeare* (Cambridge, 1986)

Studies of *Hamlet*

Eliot, T S, 'Hamlet', in *Selected Essays 1917–1932* (London, 1932)

Jump, J (ed.), *Hamlet* (Macmillan Casebook; London, 1968)

Jones, E, *Hamlet and Oedipus* (London, 1949)

Lewis, C S, 'Hamlet: The Prince or the Poem?' (Annual Shakespeare Lecture of the British Academy; London 1942);

reprinted in L D Lerner (ed.), *Shakespeare's Tragedies* (Harmondsworth, 1963)

Rose, J, 'Sexuality in the Reading of Shakespeare: *Hamlet* and *Measure for Measure*', in J Drakakis (ed.), *Alternative Shakespeares* (London, 1985)

Weitz, M, *'Hamlet' and the Philosophy of Literary Criticism* (London, 1972)